MYSTI

MYSTIC ISLE SERIES

Patricia Rice

Book View
Café

Mystic Isle

This is a work of fiction. Any references to historical events, real people, or real locales are used fictitiously. Other names, characters, places, and incidents are the product of the author's imagination, and any resemblance to actual events or locales or persons, living or dead, is entirely coincidental.

Other Book View Café books by Patricia Rice

Mysteries:
Evil Genius, *A Family Genius Mystery,* Volume 1
Undercover Genius, *A Family Genius Mystery,* Volume 2

Historical Romance:
Notorious Atherton, *The Rebellious Sons,* Volume 3
The Marquess, *Regency Nobles,* Volume 1
English Heiress, *Regency Nobles,* Volume 2
Irish Duchess, *Regency Nobles,* Volume 3

Paranormal Romance:
Trouble with Air and Magic, *The California Malcolms*

One

Kneeling at the altar, Tasia Olympus lifted the sacred chalice above her head and trembled at the terrible power she held in her hands. At the inconceivable age of twenty-five, she was responsible for every person on this island.

Still shaken by the unexpected death of their beloved priestess and grieving, she did not feel capable of caring for a kitten without Alexandra's wisdom to guide her. Her teacher had wrapped herself in confidence as if it were a golden robe. Tasia felt as if she stood naked in her ignorance.

Facing the altar, with her back to the kneeling acolytes, Tasia hid her terror from their sight and concentrated on the familiar ceremony. Behind her, Sirene the Musician's high clear voice echoed against the temple's tall marble columns in celebration of the moment—Tasia's installation as the new priestess. Sunshine poured through the open portico. Dust motes filtered through the rays, dancing past the beautifully carved frieze of the goddess and her servants.

In the security of this ordinary routine, she trustingly opened her mind's eye, hoping for Aelynn's blessing. Instead, she was instantly blinded to all but her inner vision. Thunderous, raging waves crashed down upon her, impossibly sweeping through the temple, tumbling the walls and friezes. High upon the protected mountain, the temple buildings drowned in a sea of water that swept away their home and all the beloved relics they held.

Gasping in horror, stunned and shaking, Tasia fled the holy vision. Clinging to the sacred chalice to steady herself, she shut her mind down before she collapsed in front of the assembly. She wanted to leap up screaming at the horrifying images in her head— even as the maidens in the temple repeated their peaceful prayers of worship, unaware of the danger ahead.

Tasia stood and silently begged Aelynn the Goddess for answers.

The altar rattled and plaster dust drifted from the frieze.

The goddess usually came to her in visions, but terrified that the earth's rumble was Aelynn's means of implying urgency, Tasia swallowed hard and prayed for guidance. The rattling stopped, and she swallowed her fear. Not yet, dear Aelynn, please, give her time to think...

The earth occasionally rumbled without causing more harm than a few cracked walls. Would anyone believe her if she said they must all abandon the only home they'd ever known with no more warning than that?

Her knees quaked as much as the chalice. And the marble altar.

And not just from her lack of courage.

More tremors. Was this how the gods meant to wreak their havoc? The time was *now*? She hadn't even finished her first ceremony.

A stone pillar crashed at the corner of the temple. The floor beneath her knees swayed, rippling like ocean waves, throwing her off balance. She lowered the chalice to cradle it protectively in her arms like a baby and turned to view the frightened faces gazing up at her for answers. Had the floor not shivered beneath her, she would be shuddering anyway at such responsibility.

Sirene's voice wavered but neither she nor the lute players halted until Tasia gestured. As if her break from routine was more frightening than the quaking earth, a babble of panic rose with the plaster dust filling the air.

Myra the frightened newcomer, only six years of age, turned trusting eyes to her Priestess. The student beside Myra had been here for most of the twelve years of her life and waited obediently for orders, serene in the belief that the priestess would provide answers. Even the women who had taught Tasia all she knew clasped hands and waited for her to assure them that all would be well—because she was the only one among them to whom the goddess spoke.

If Tasia had interpreted her vision correctly—all would *not* be well. Change and upheaval and terrible danger were their future. An impossible future. The temple sat high upon an enormous hill. No wave could conceivably reach it—but she must trust Aelynn. This must be a test of her obedience.

Her stomach clenched in dread. She loved her safe, stable

home. How could she abandon all she knew with only these images in her head telling her to go?

The shaking pillars answered for her.

Tasia clung to the altar to steady herself against the rocking of the once-solid ground. In her fear, she could scarcely speak. Her first task as priestess would destroy the very foundations of Aelynn's believers and demand unimaginable loyalty.

"We must all take the boats to the shore," she instructed the nearest teacher, trying to sound calm and assured, like Alexandra ordering a new scroll. Bringing down the authority of Aelynn would add to the panic, so she needed to sound confident in her commands. "Please have your students fetch those who are not present and tell them to follow us to the galleys. I have *Seen* the future."

Her older vestals were watching her with alarm, but pronouncements of visions and unruffled orders reassured the youngest girls of her omnipotence. Tasia remembered a time when the whole world was a mystery in which she must trust the adults who governed her life. She had thought she'd gain confidence with maturity. Instead, she had only added more doubts.

For the sake of her acolytes, she humbly thanked Aelynn for choosing to send the vision during this particular ceremony.

For Tasia's first appearance as priestess, the vestals in this initial audience had brought symbols of their various trades for blessing. Teachers clung to precious scrolls. Cook clung to her ladle. Gaia held her hoe. For the second blessing, the Healer would be gathering her herb seeds, and others, with their students, would be choosing their most precious tools.

The second ceremony wouldn't happen today. At Tasia's announcement, messengers scurried into the spring sunlight, fleeing the temple, racing down the many stairs to the various outbuildings.

The older vestals watched Tasia with uncertainty. She was young and inexperienced. Her visions had always been filtered through Alexandra's interpretations. Those were reasons enough to question Tasia's leadership. Still, her vestals had to obey or forsake the goddess they worshipped.

Daskala, one of her best teachers, opened her mouth to question, an unthinkable disobedience under Alexandra's tenure. Tasia pointed at the door, refusing argument.

The ground rumbled, groaned, and cracked. The reluctant remainder of her small congregation fled.

Outside, through the terraced gardens, her messengers raced from kitchen to sickroom to classroom, warning the workers who had waited for the second blessing. Tasia hurried down the steep steps in the wake of her flock, counting heads as women poured from the outbuildings carrying whatever they had at hand when called.

All told, the goddess had barely three dozen virgins worshipping her in these heathen times, and many of them were too young for understanding. Once, the temple had housed dozens of adults and few children. War and famine had changed life on the mainland, along with their belief in a peace-loving goddess.

The ground continued to tremble as if they walked a terrible battleground of the gods. Women and children raced down the marble stairs to the top of the cliff path—a path they had not traversed since their first arrival. Tasia hurried after them, still counting heads.

A long crack opened in the steps down the slope. Children screamed. The acolytes only used this stairway to leave their requests with the sailors below, or to pick up the supplies the men hauled up for their use. Her maidens had not talked to men since they'd been brought to the temple.

As Tasia watched, loose rocks fell loose from the bluff's edge and tumbled to the sea below. They would all be flung to their deaths if they did not hurry.

"Where is Khaos?" Tasia asked urgently when her count came up one head short.

"She ran back to the schoolroom. I do not know why," called Daskala, shepherding the youngest to the last set of stairs to the bluff. "She is old enough to find her own way."

Not if a pediment fell on her. Torn between carrying the precious chalice to safety and leading a single—very mischievous—child behind, Tasia wished for the more experienced Alexandra to tell her what to do.

The rumbling abruptly ceased, but Tasha knew it would return—bringing worse destruction if her vision was to be believed. Lacking any other knowledge of their fates, Tasia had to trust her interpretation.

The chalice must be saved at all costs, but she could not leave a child behind. And she could not send one of the women in her care into danger. Although as leader, she should be the first to share words with the men to whom they never spoke, Tasia still could not give up the child.

In desperation, she handed the sacred vessel to Charis, the small woman who acted as caretaker for the priestess.

"Please, if they ask, you must tell the soldiers to man both boats and fill them with supplies. I will be right back."

Short, dark, and cross-eyed, humble Charis looked stunned and awed to be given such responsibility, but Tasia had grown up with her. Charis had never let her down.

Another pillar in the temple above crashed as Tasia lifted her best tunic and ran back up the cracking stairs. For her inaugural ceremony, she had been wearing her newest sandals, the leather still stiff and difficult to tie. Grabbing stone walls to keep from sliding, she prayed to Aelynn that the ties wouldn't come undone.

Below, she heard masculine shouts as the soldiers saw the vestals pouring down the bluff from the temple high ground. The women never descended to the shore. There were strict rules keeping the sexes apart. She needed to be there to keep order. By all that was holy, why had Aelynn taken Alexandra and left the burden in her inexperienced hands?

Tasia kept running uphill against the recurring tremors. She gasped at the stitch in her side, and then in relief. Seemingly unharmed, Khaos rushed toward her, carrying heavy burlap sacks over each shoulder.

Not wasting time asking questions, Tasia took one of the sacks from the thirteen-year-old. "The boats cannot hold much," she warned.

The ground began to shake again, harder this time.

"The roof fell. I could not leave the scrolls unprotected," Khaos called over her shoulder, leaping down the steps with the sureness of a mountain goat.

The stairs over the bluff and down the cliff had never been even. Now, the stones had cracked and parted with the earth's tremors.

They did not speak again as the ground did its best to heave them airborne or bury them in boulders and dust. Women were screaming and men shouting by the time Tasia slid the last meter or two to the sand.

She twisted her ankle and stumbled trying to right herself from her undignified fall. A tall soldier with fair hair darker than her own caught her. His big, callused hand was foreign to her, and she jerked away as quickly as she could.

He wore a short jeweled sword and dagger in his belt, and she shivered at his masculine touch. She had not seen a man since her father had left her with the priestess years ago, when she was scarcely old enough to remember. She had not spoken to a man since. Her tongue was tied.

Not suffering the same impediment, he steadied her elbow. "Let me take that." He heaved the heavy bag over his shoulder. "You are the priestess?" he asked, apparently identifying the purple and gold belt girdling her midsection. "I am Nautilus, captain of your soldiers, at your command."

The soldiers guarded the island, providing the island's only contact with the rest of the world. They prevented worshippers from climbing the stairs and bothering the vestals. They accepted the offerings to Aelynn—and often the unwanted children. They tended the flocks of sheep and goats and fished from the sea to provide food the acolytes could not grow for themselves.

They also sailed the channel to bring back other goods the island could not produce on its own. But the men never spoke with Aelynn's vestals. This one did not seem bothered by that detail.

The captain was large, so much larger than she had imagined. He smelled...male, not scented as her maidens were. His bronzed bare biceps glistened with the sweat of some exertion—he must have the strength of a god. They would need his strength, so she must not show her fear to one who could break her in two with his bare hands.

As priestess, she was in charge of the women. As representative of the state on the mainland, the captain was in charge of his men. Their authority had never crossed before. She had to assert hers now, for the sake of Aelynn. She pictured Alexandra speaking with authority and used the same tone, so as to hide her uncertainty.

"Great waves are coming," she warned, limping toward the women huddled on the beach, each still carrying what she'd held last. "We must abandon the island and seek safety on the mainland, far into the hills. All the villages on the coast will be destroyed."

His expression neutral, he nodded acknowledgment of her command. "The sea is restless when the earth trembles. We'll take your galley."

"We need both boats," she insisted, seeing them sitting on the beach. "We must take everyone and everything."

"We haven't enough crew to man two heavy boats. Leave your possessions here," he ordered. He dropped the scrolls and turned away to shout orders.

Tasia picked up the scrolls again. "We take both boats and everything they can carry," she countermanded. She might doubt her ability to lead, but she did not doubt Aelynn's order to take all they could carry.

"There is no time," he argued. "Things can be replaced, not people."

Tasia had seldom argued with anyone, and most certainly not a soldier who knew a great deal more of the world than she. She could not even imagine how those frail galleys could float on the pounding surf.

But the goddess had spoken and must be obeyed. She'd watched Alexandra for decades and knew how a priestess must conduct herself. This time, rather than acknowledge that she was arguing with a terrifying male stranger, she used the tone Alexandra would have used with a cross neophyte.

"To save people, we will need our things," she said sharply. "Food, supplies, everything we can fit into *both* galleys. The goddess commands us."

"I've heard of the great waves following the earth's quaking," the captain argued, undeterred by her command. "The sea gods are stronger than your goddess. If they are angry, leaving now is more important."

Even as Alexandra's assistant, she'd never been brushed aside so completely. He rattled her confidence, but she could not let him undermine Aelynn's orders.

Already, the men were dragging a lone galley to the water. Boys herded goats and chickens to the shore. Avoiding the unfamiliar men, her women filled vessels at the well. So many people dependent on them, looking frail in comparison to the endless surf churning on the shore.

"The worst quake is far from here. We are only feeling a small part of it," she told the captain, as if he were a slow student. "The danger is tremendous. Surviving once we reach solid land is as important as escaping the island. Villages will be destroyed. We cannot know how long we will be gone. We need both galleys and all they can hold. The goddess commands," she repeated with stern emphasis.

He glared, as if he meant to question her visions or the goddess. But duty bound to protect her, he had to accept her insistence on a larger scale of security. Obviously struggling with impatience, he shouted instructions to his sailors, and they raced to haul out the second galley.

Relieved that she did not need to waste more time arguing with a giant of a man whose authority and worldliness intimidated her, Tasia limped up and down the sand, dividing the women and children between the boats. She reassured the youngest and issued quiet commands to the older ones. She lifted a questioning eyebrow to Charis, who nodded at the long boat adorned with the royal purple and gold of the goddess. The chalice was safely inside.

The sunny day gradually disappeared behind thunderous clouds on the horizon. Increasingly large waves splashed against the rocky beach. An earthquake and now a storm...

"We have loaded two days of supplies," Captain Nautilus said tightly. "Will that satisfy the goddess?"

She shivered in fear as she noticed that the usual noisy seabirds had disappeared from the shore. "Have we loaded all the food stores?"

"The ships are carrying grain as ballast. We have olives, crates of lemons. Our root vegetables are almost gone this time of year. We have the cargo of pigs and goats we were about to trade."

"Take anything we can. There will be nothing left..." Her words fell away on a whisper of grief.

Glancing toward the gleaming white temple and buildings on the crest of the high hill that had been her home, Tasia fought back tears. This was the end of the world as she knew it. She tried to memorize each tall palm, every olive bush, the color of the lemons against the leaves...

"It's a strong temple," the captain said reassuringly. "It will be here when you return."

"No, it will not," she said sadly.

* * *

Nautilus brushed off the priestess's dire prediction. Women cultivated pessimism at the best of times. Priestesses needed to uphold their grandiose reputations by offering grim warnings. Then when the predictions didn't materialize, they could crow that the goddess had saved them.

The highest waves of an ocean wouldn't reach that hill, and this was a mere sea. But with the earth shaking beneath their feet and a storm moving in, it was not the best time to argue over the impossible with an unworldly, terrified woman accustomed to having her every wish fulfilled.

He'd never met any of the priestesses, but he'd heard the last one was elderly. This one most definitely was not. Her hair was a rare white-blond, and her form was all graceful curves. She barely looked old enough to teach a schoolroom.

If she truly believed the tide would destroy them, it was his duty to keep her calm. The quaking earth was the least of their worries if he had a ship full of hysterical women.

The gold in his pocket didn't come from a goddess, but from the state that paid him to protect the vestals—even from themselves, if necessary.

Bowing to her command in this, Nautilus left Lady Tasia to her charges. He stalked up and down the beach, balancing loads and crews between the two galleys. He cursed the slowness required for this large an expedition, and cursed his men for stumbling over their own feet while stealing looks at the maidens. If they must leave this safe port, they needed to be sailing *now*.

The younger boys were trying to be brave, but the excitement was too much for them. Some were weeping. Others were simply underfoot.

To his relief, a cross-eyed vestal ushered the more excitable into the care of several seemingly steadier older girls. Startled to be in the company of a mother figure, the boys settled down. With a task to perform, the girls lost their anxious expressions and set about finding places for their charges.

Nautilus hoped they could reach the mainland before the waves worsened, if they worsened. Already, the tremors had slowed. He cast a glance to the lowering clouds. It would make a nice break in his duties to spend a mighty storm in the arms of the raven-haired beauty to whom he'd been promised.

Someday soon, he'd have the home and family he'd worked so hard to achieve. He had the gold, he had a chosen wife, and her family would welcome his trading skills. All he needed was to finish these last months of his obligation to the temple guard.

When he could do no more, when the priestess had turned so pale and her sea-blue eyes had grown so wide that she looked as if she might expire of terror, Nautilus ordered the boats out of the harbor.

"Have you sailed before?" he asked, steering the priestess in the direction of the hatch.

She shook her head. "Not since I was a child too young to remember."

"The distance to the mainland is not great once we leave the harbor and sail past the curve in the island." He nodded toward the outcropping of land that protected the island harbor.

Only then did it occur to him that if she'd been on that hill since infancy, she'd never spoken to a man. Half her terror was no doubt of him and his men. Mentally cursing his obtuseness, he bowed and strode away so as not to frighten her more.

He checked the billowing clouds on the distant horizon. They should have time to reach the village before the worst of the storm struck, thank Poseidon. Inexperienced sailors like the women could wreak havoc if forced to sail too long in turbulent water.

He turned his attention to the mighty sea, expecting whitecaps. Instead...the sea was unnaturally retreating from shore

He had heard of the mighty waves produced by an earthquake, but he'd never seen such a tide. He'd not believe the tales...except he didn't like this strange phenomenon. Could the priestess have sensed the waves better than he had?

His pulse beat a little faster, and he barked curt orders to his crew. Reacting to his urgency, the last of his men shoved the galley deeper into the water and jumped over the bow just as the sails opened.

The priestess, too, spoke to her women, sending them below with the children, watching the other galley anxiously. But she did not leave the deck. She settled on a bench and clutched her arms, watching as Nautilus commanded the sails to be unfurled. The lady was as beautiful as any goddess and needed to be out of sight. Her behavior was as maddening as any mortal female's.

Having been raised among men, he consider women interchangeable, but this one...maintained a dignity despite her panic, a poise he'd not noticed in any but the highest authorities—who were never women.

Until now, none of his crew had ever spoken directly with the women on the mountain. The temple sent messages over the bluff via a rope lift when the inhabitants required anything. His duty was to provide what they needed, and he had always been in charge of how it was done.

He was unaccustomed to having his orders overruled by anyone, dignified, beautiful, or otherwise.

"The storm is moving in; we should have whitecaps," Demetri, his first mate said as Nautilus took his place at the stern.

"The lack of wind is unnatural," Nautilus agreed. Anxious to gain sight of the mainland, he signaled for full sail. "Without wind or tide, we can't row these heavy loads."

Nautilus studied the lap of the waters against the galley bobbing behind them. "We'll need to go deeper and hope for a breeze." He nodded to a darker blue current outside their normal route. "We can't reach the village from there. We'd best aim for the fort."

A wave rolled the galley, and one of the women screamed.

"The vestals are poor sailors," Demetri warned. "We need to land as quickly as we can. Hysteria will spread if not nipped in the bud."

Cursing under his breath, Nautilus debated sending Demetri to settle the screamer. Before he could do so, the priestess sent her cross-eyed handmaiden below. A moment later, the screaming stopped, he noted in relief.

"West," Nautilus shouted to his oarsmen after testing the winds and his other senses. "To the fort!"

The fort was farther than the village, but a more direct route to the west, out of the storm's path. Built on a natural harbor formed by a high barrier of boulders, the fort should keep them safe from high tides.

As they rowed away from the island, into the sea, the current abruptly changed and wind filled the sails, rapidly carrying them away from the coast.

A crash echoed over the waters, and the crew halted in horror.

The mainland heaved as if giants stomped across the countryside in anger. Trees toppled into splinters. The columns of the city's acropolis fractured, bent, and smashed in a smoky haze of dust. Smaller structures crumbled as the earth heaved and cracked—letting in the sea.

Like ants, people swarmed around the distant structures, scurrying down the streets carrying their possessions on their backs or in barrows and carts. They raced for the distant hills—for better reason than crashing pilasters.

As Nautilus watched in horror, the mirror-like tide was followed by an enormous wave so high that the ocean trembled.

The storm wind caught the sails and raced the galleys in an opposite direction from the mighty wave. All Nautilus could do was watch in disbelief as the powerful wave broke over the island, drowning the temple on its mountain. It continued onward, roaring in a turbulent wall of water that smacked high against the mainland. The bluff the village was built on slid into the waves, taking the pier, the warehouses, and all the boats with it. What had survived the quake now floated out to sea in splinters.

Nautilus saw the destruction with horror. All the jolly women with whom he'd flirted, the men he'd come to respect, the woman he'd hoped to marry... He prayed they'd escaped with their lives, but their homes and livelihoods were demolished—along with all his hopes of a wealthy, contented life in an established community. With no harbor, there could be no village again.

He conquered the urge to steer against the current, to seek the family he'd wished to marry into. But it was a fool's notion to fight the sea. The people in the village had had time to flee. He could not help them, and he had over six dozen people and his ships to save.

He turned his eyes ahead, only to watch the indestructible fort on the promontory smashed by the tide and crumble beneath the tremors. Columns fell, roofs crashed. Waves beat higher than the boulders that had once offered them safety.

Hot lead sat in the pit of Nautilus's belly—the priestess had been *right*? It was all gone?

The women who stayed on deck wept and keened. The priestess spoke sharply and ordered them below to care for the children.

Nautilus kept staring in disbelief at the land that was no longer there. Bits of debris bobbed in the water, tossed by the storm moving in and the rip tide forming from the impossible surf.

"Further west?" Styros, one of his sailors, asked in shock as he gazed to the flooded mainland.

"If the wind and current hold," Nautilus agreed, hiding his trepidation. Once they passed where the fort had been, they were sailing into enemy waters, at risk of pirates and Romans—with nowhere safe to land.

He caught the eye of the priestess. Instead of sitting on her throne, she now stood with one arm circling the mast, straining to see the shore, her expression one of taut restraint as she watched the mainland turn into sea.

The wind tore at her white blond hair, freeing it from her headpiece. Her robes clung to every shapely curve. Nautilus knew it was a sin to think lustful thoughts of the women he'd been sworn to protect, women who'd given themselves to the goddess, but he was a man, one long denied the comfort of prostitutes ashore. Sin and nature went hand in hand.

The lady caught his eye and nodded worriedly at the bend of the shore ahead. There was no fort beyond that point, no civilization. Still, they had little choice but to outrun the quakes and waves. He nodded acknowledgment that they would have to sail further into the sea and not to shore.

With a look of despair, she glanced back to the place where land should be, then accepted the aid of one of her handmaidens to go below. Nautilus breathed easier having her safely out of sight.

Dark was closing in. The sea was increasingly tempestuous as the force of the enormous tide spread. He prayed for safety.

The next tidal wave struck before they passed the battered fort.

* * *

Tasia grabbed the smallest girl and flattened the child beneath her, yelling at her other vestals to do the same. As the women covered the children with their bodies, the galley rose out of the sea. A wave flung it as if the long ship was no more than driftwood.

Around her, women and men alike wept and prayed. The boat went airborne, making it impossible for the men to row. It hit the water again, still upright, only to be carried high again.

Fighting her terror, Tasia found strength in Aelynn. She prayed aloud, placing the boats and their occupants in the hands of the goddess. Even the sailors joined in her fervent prayers as their oars struck water and pushed them past the next roll of water to the trough in between.

The instant the ship stopped its wild leaps and dives and the men manned the oars again, Tasia hastened above to speak with the captain.

Fog had set in. The temple island was no longer visible, hadn't been since that first wave of water. Her heart sunk to the soles of her new sandals.

Worse, in this fog, the second boat was no longer in sight. Half their people were on that boat, and her heart cried despairingly to Aelynn. Through the moist miasma, she could hear Captain Nautilus shouting orders, trying to keep his crew calm. But their panic was almost palpable.

She had heard whispers of sea monsters. The sea itself was a monster as far as she could tell, but this was not the time to express fear. Fear was their enemy. How would Alexandra handle a moment like this?

In shock, Tasia realized the vestals had always buffered the elderly priestess from emergencies, except to ask for her help in prayer. Swallowing her terror at realizing she had no example to fall back on, Tasia drew on her own need for security.

"Aelynn has blessed us!" she cried through the damp murk, hoping this would give everyone courage as the boats crossed another swell. "We are saved from the mighty tide! All hail Aelynn!"

Her cry carried through the gloom. The other women picked up the familiar chant. Sirene sang her musical version of the prayer.

Over a brief calm, they could hear the women on the other galley pick up the chant. The others were alive!

She could not ask for more. Heart pounding, she dropped to her knees in thanksgiving.

The Captain shouted his commands. The oarsmen struck up a rhythm in accompaniment to the chant. Tasia adapted her prayers to the strokes of the men trying to stay abreast of the strong current.

Behind them, she could see nothing of the island they had left— or the mainland they'd hoped to reach. Huge waves rose and fell as far as the eye could see.

Two

Late that evening, after the storm lightened, Nautilus spooned up the mush that had been created with their limited stores and no fire. With his sailor's strong instincts, he watched for a glimpse of stars through the thick clouds and thicker fog. He had not sailed this far beyond the Greek islands since his youth.

"Perhaps we could turn back now?" Styros suggested. A sailor who'd lost his hand in a pirate attack, he knew these waters as well as Nautilus, knew the treachery on every coast they passed.

"I'm fairly certain the wind has blown us into the Ionian," Nautilus admitted with a pang of deep sorrow. This sea was even more turbulent than the protected Aegean. He'd hoped after thirty years at sea, he might finally settle down, but there could be no turning back until the wind and water calmed.

Instead, another major storm was brewing, if he was any judge at all. He held up his finger to the wind and nodded at the current. "The wind and tide are against us. Even if they weren't, we could only hope to return to devastation and debris that would sink us. We have to sail south and hope the wind and waves favor us come morning. You have sailed this sea. What are our chances?"

"Not favorable," Styros agreed in resignation. "We're heading toward Sicily, where the war rages on. We can't port there. Do you know any safe harbors until we can turn back?"

"Massalia," Nautilus said, after giving it some thought. "Small and very far to the west, but our countrymen have settled there."

He did not express his greatest fears—that they would never be able to return to Greece, that the destruction they'd seen was worse than the priestess's dire warnings. That he suggested a port of Greek colonists beyond the spreading Roman empire said all he dared say.

As if she'd heard his thoughts, the priestess stepped from the shadows. "The gods have not favored Greece these last years. The world is changing. I have Seen it."

"What can you know of the wars of men, sheltered as you are?" Nautilus asked, grumpier and less respectful than he should have been. Had she allowed him to take only the one ship, he wouldn't be worrying about the others now.

"I know very little of the world," she admitted. "But the goddess lets me See the strife and hunger, the droughts and storms. Since I am powerless, it is not always useful information. Once, kings came to peaceful Aelynn to beg our favor. No longer. Now they turn to war gods."

"The world does change, my lady. Sometimes, I am sorry for it." Nautilus bowed his head in acknowledgment, although his interest was captured more in her fair form than the topic. In his experience, nothing stopped change. One just took advantage of the opportunities that arose.

Opportunity stood before him. Thinking of the virgin priestess in his bed was not just disrespectful, but heretical. Still—they had no temple, no island to protect. What was a priestess without a temple and worshippers? *Opportunity,* whispered through his mind.

"You are not *always* sorry," she said haughtily, understanding his modifier—or his mood.

The lady was more clever than her beauty should allow. He didn't want to acknowledge that because *respect* stood in the way of opportunity.

She seemed ready to say more, but the waves swelled beneath their feet. The wind took a blustery cold direction that puffed the sails and threw the oarsmen off balance.

"I will do my best to keep us safe, my lady," Nautilus promised.

"The other galley?" she asked in concern. The other ship had disappeared in the fog. They could no longer even hear them. "Is there any hope we'll see them again?"

"Pray to your goddess," he answered cynically, hiding his despair. He had good friends and brave young boys on the other ship. They'd be with him now had she listened. Before he was forced into a wasted argument, he walked away to change their course to a less dangerous one.

Despite the increasing storm winds whipping the sails, an unnatural fog closed in. Without the stars to guide them, all they could do was hold on and pray to stay upright.

The women took turns chanting their prayers, sleeping, keeping the children settled, and preparing what nourishment could be provided without heat.

On the brisk sea breeze, Nautilus inhaled scents he didn't recognize. His senses had been trained to identify his position from sight and sound and smell. He hoped it was the women diverting his instincts. He feared it was not.

His instincts warned: *Ahead, there be dragons.*

* * *

Two more days of black clouds, two nights of heavy fog, and everyone was weary, hungry, thirsty, and terrified. Those children who weren't seasick cried themselves to sleep at night. The women prayed and, like Tasia, helped the ill.

Prayer wasn't enough to stop fever from spreading. One of the sailors helped carry six-year-old Myra to the deck where Tasia hoped the breezes might cool the child. Kneeling beside the sick acolyte, she spooned water past Myra's dry lips, trying not to spill a single precious drop.

At a shout from the prow, Tasia wearily glanced up. Through the heavy dawn fog, she could see little except the captain standing high above the others. His metal arm bands caught a glint of sun.

Sun? She gazed behind them, to the east. On the horizon, a single beam of light seeped through a thin break in the heavy gloom. A lone seabird circled against the piece of blue. She prayed fervently to the goddess and searched for any sight of the second ship.

She saw nothing—literally and figuratively. The fog still hung on the water—and the goddess sent her no vision of their fate. Tasia's heart was as heavy as the moisture-laden haze sealing them off from the world.

"Rocks ahoy!" one of the sailors shouted.

Tasia could sense the crew's unease at this cry. The rowers stopped hauling on their oars, waiting for further command. The sail flapped limply without a breeze to feed it.

If there was land, she longed to be on it. She hated being buffeted by the winds and waves of fate. She needed solid ground to stand on. And so did the women in her care—women who relied on her for everything. Everyone turned toward the prow, hopeful that rocks meant land.

The patch of blue widened above the distant eastern horizon behind them, but the pale light failed to illuminate the dense layer of fog ahead. Moisture muted their surroundings. In the eerie silence, even the waves lapped noiselessly.

"Rocks may mean land, or they may mean submerged dangers to crash against," one of the captain's men explained when she questioned. "We are not familiar with this shore. The captain sailed with his father while a boy. He is the widest traveled of us. I do not envy his decision now."

Tasia handed the water to another acolyte and rose, straightening her crumpled tunic. She had learned to walk on a wildly pitching deck, but she had scarcely slept in two days. Her knees were weak. She could not let her character be the same. She worked her way forward to where Nautilus stood on the prow, a ray of golden sunshine highlighting his yellow hair. He stood tall on the upper deck, and the sun appeared to seek him out despite the thick gloom.

Except for the captain, Tasia could see no more than the swirling gray clouds of fog. Be there dragons, pirates, or rocks ahead, they had no choice except to look for land or die at sea.

"The goddess has brought us to shelter," she stated firmly, standing beside the captain, straining to see just a glimpse of green. "The Chalice will bring us Plenty, as promised."

"We are likely to founder on the rocks and bring plenty to the fishes," he argued. "I see no safe harbor, nothing but high cliffs. We'll have to sail around."

"I cannot see your cliffs," she said in puzzlement. The captain must have the eyes of a bird or the guidance skills of a fish in water.

"My vision is external. The visions your goddess sends is internal," he suggested. "I hear the waves against high rocks, smell the salt, feel the cliffs blocking the wind. This place is not on the map I know in my head. I have no idea how far from the mainland we have blown. I do not even know for certain which sea we sail."

"We are low on drinking water," she reminded him. "Surely there is some way of finding a harbor where we could explore."

"Rocks do not provide water. No disrespect, lady," the stubborn captain retorted, "but my task is to sail us to safety. Yours is to tend to our souls."

Tasia had not been raised to anger, but she had the urge to slap this arrogant man who fought her every request. "Your theology is not mine, then," she said coldly. "My task is to be a vessel for Aelynn, grant her wishes that she may bless her worshippers. And to that end, I must care for her acolytes, and they need water. There is fever. It will spread unless the ill can be isolated. Please, let us land. There might be water even on rocks."

The golden sailor frowned, held up his hand for silence, and listened to the birds. Or the breeze. Or to the air blowing between his ears for all Tasia knew. She had little knowledge of men and soldiers. She had aided Alexandra these last years, though, and had some knowledge of authority. It was heeded best when backed with experience, and she had none.

The captain gestured for the sail to be furled. Another order had the men rowing one stroke at a time, testing the rocky but fog-concealed walls that the man in the bow swore rose around them.

As the sun climbed higher, the fog grew thinner. Now Tasia could see the formidable cliffs defining the narrow channel they sailed. The women gasped in awe and shivered in fear as the oars hit upon solid stone beneath the water and shoved away. Maintaining her stoic expression, Tasia strained to see ahead.

"Can we be trapped in here?" she murmured to the captain.

"If we can row in, we should be able to row out." He hesitated, as if leaving something unsaid.

Tasia considered all the possibilities of pirates and brigands and enemy soldiers and was happy not to have any of her fears confirmed. She bowed her head and prayed fervently.

As if understanding her needs, Charis approached bearing the chalice in her arms. In relief, Tasia lifted the sacred object above her head and hailed the goddess. High above the rocky shadows, the dawn's light blessed the gold.

Aloud, she gave prayers of thanks to Aelynn for leading them from danger and imploring Her aid in bringing them to safety. Sirene accompanied her prayers with songs of thanksgiving.

As if strengthened by the certainty of the women, the men rowed with more enthusiasm, maneuvering a channel they could only sense through the heavy moist air and deep shadows.

"Aelynn, bestow your blessings upon all these good men and women," Tasia chanted.

A rumble and shudder not unlike that of the land they left behind sloshed the waves on deck. Women screamed. Nautilus looked grim.

And then, as if Aelynn heeded her call, the fog lifted and the shadows parted. The sweet scent of lemon trees tickled her nose. And the galley glided into a wide natural harbor of crystalline blue waters and a black sand beach. A rock bluff rose high above the north side of the U-shaped harbor. The beach at the center of the waterfront gradually sloped upward to where tall palms danced in a breeze. In the far distance, well above the trees, loomed a high mountain surrounded by fog, steam, or smoke. Tasia couldn't quite tell.

Undisturbed vegetation lined the shoreline and beach. No cook fires smoked. No paths indicated animal or man trampling down to enjoy the gentle surf. Not a single building marred the pristine landscape.

"Volcano," Nautilus ventured. "We've found a volcanic island."

"You have seen these before?" she asked, studying the smoking mountain with trepidation.

"There are many islands like this. Most are not habitable."

"But this one is," she breathed in triumph, gazing at the trees lining the black beach. "Aelynn has brought us to safety."

As the rowers took them closer to shore, and no pirates or monsters appeared to greet them, her words couldn't be refuted. But Nautilus looked unconvinced as he gave orders to land the galley.

They sailed safely into the natural port, but gazes constantly swiveled to search the narrow aperture they'd just navigated, watching for the second boat.

Even if the others were still alive, how could they possibly find their way through such a hidden passage?

* * *

The men Nautilus sent into the interior of the island returned with jugs of spring water and edible fruit they'd scavenged from trees and plants. Their efforts were rewarded by shy smiles from some of the women and enthusiasm from the children.

Others of the crew fished the harbor and provided for their evening meal. The women used their spare herbs and few tools to cook the fish. The crew carried the ship's supplies to shores, and the acolytes fried flatbread and roasted vegetables over fires struck from the sailor's flint boxes.

Together, forgetting some of their awkwardness in their haste to create shelter, both the acolytes and sailors learned to weave palm fronds around poles to create temporary roofs.

Aelynn had provided, indeed. The next morning, Nautilus surveyed the impromptu camp with approval—and doubt. For now, his crew was in awe of the virtuous servants of a goddess, and the acolytes were intimidated by hairy, rough men. They simply worked together to provide necessities.

In a day or two, reality would sink in. The men would realize that if they stayed here, they were foresworn not to touch the virgins, but there was no one to pay them for their obedience. They would want to leave, but to where and what? All they knew had been destroyed.

No willing women waited for them in a lively village filled with opportunity to invest their gold. The crew had brought their money pouches with them, but what good were coins without civilization? They would have to leave this island to spend them, and for all they knew, they were surrounded by pirates and warring Romans.

In the meantime, the ill had to be tended. They'd been isolated in their own shelter on the far side of the black sand beach, where several of the vestals cared for them. The women had even provided a bed for injured and feverish crew—which kept grumblings to a minimum. Had the women expected to be waited on, his crew would be plotting their escape already.

Groups of men and women set out together to search the interior. Nautilus set a few of his crew to guarding the encampment and others to rest.

He couldn't rest while half his men were lost.

He sought the priestess and found her with the ill. She handed over her duties to another, rose, and led him into the shelter of trees.

"We must find some way of separating the men and women," she said with a weary sigh, "but I haven't the strength for it now. Is there some way you can order your men to keep their distance?

"For the moment, they're working well together. My men are duty bound to protect your maidens— until such time as they realize we are here without the authority of church or state to guide or pay us," Nautilus said cynically. "Prayers can only do so much against temptation."

She winced and nodded wearily, and he was sorry for his cruel words. She was much too sheltered to understand the temptation of dozens of women. He'd have to handle his crew.

"Aelynn's teachings promise that we shall have plenty so long as we shall be like children unto her. She has always provided bounty, as you can see from this island." She gestured at the rich land spreading as far as the eye could see. "Our sacred chalice is called the Chalice of Plenty, a gift directly from the gods. We must uphold her laws or risk losing all. I have not been given any insight on how to deal with temptation."

A temptation the isolated maidens had never known, Nautilus thought. The women were as human as his men.

The young musician with the haunting voice hesitated at the edge of the clearing, obviously waiting for her priestess. Nautilus gestured toward her, and the lady raised a questioning eyebrow. "Yes, Sirene?"

"Since Mageiras isn't here to cook, I thought I might help," the musician said tentatively. "Heron has offered to teach me how to use a spare flint box to start the fire, so we need not wait for the men to provide us. Do I have your permission to work with him?"

Nautilus knew his lieutenant wished to help where he could, but the man also had an eye for a beautiful woman, and the musician was lovely. He refrained from commenting as the priestess hesitated, then reluctantly agreed. "We should all learn as much from each other as we can," she admitted. "There are no other cook fires to borrow from in this place."

Not knowing how near the mainland might be, nor who inhabited it, self-sufficiency was necessary for their immediate survival. Nautilus approved of her decision but knew she did not understand the bonds that developed between people who worked together. He hoped her goddess was an understanding one.

"How do we seek the other galley?" the lady asked after the musician departed. "Once we're all together again, we can plan."

"That was the reason I sought you out," he said in relief that she understood. "I need to sail out and find a way of signaling them. We also need to mark the entrance so we can find it again. We will need oil to set rushes burning. Your chalice has provided so much, dare we ask its blessing to steer our comrades to our door?"

It wasn't as if he actually believed the goddess had provided, but his men needed belief in more than a mortal captain. He hated to ask more of this frail female. Her head barely reached his shoulders.

Dark circles rimmed the fair skin around her eyes. She must have been up all night working with the ill and hadn't taken time to fasten loosened strands of white-blond hair. Wisps blew around her face and throat like gossamer threads.

But at his request, she straightened her spine with the firmness of iron and spoke with authority. "We will hold a brief ceremony and prayers if your men can build a small altar in a protected place. When do you need to sail?"

She was stronger than he'd thought, and her mind clearly followed his own. Had she been any other woman...he would have kissed her in gratitude.

"We need to sail when the tide turns at daybreak. Will a tree trunk suffice as altar until we return?"

She nodded acceptance. "I will find a place where my vestals can gather. Your men will need to stay outside of the area, but their prayers are always welcome."

"Does Aelynn require sacrifices?" Nautilus asked warily. "We have little to give."

She closed her eyes and appeared to drift off to sleep while she stood there. Nautilus frowned, prepared to catch her if she toppled over. He feared being struck by lightning for touching a priestess, but he couldn't bear to see her harmed.

Oddly, as she swayed, he felt as if another force entered the clearing, an invisible one that encompassed the priestess and brushed impatiently at him for daring nearness. He stepped back in surprise. Did she truly gain her strength from some unseen element?

He was superstitious enough about his own instincts to believe they were provided by Poseidon. Perhaps the lady's instincts came from air.

Her lids fluttered. She shook herself, seemed to glance around to remember where she was, and nodded. "I think in our case, work is the sacrifice. Aelynn's vestals have specific duties they have learned, but they are not all useful at times like these. If we are to stay here for long, we must all take on tasks for which we are not trained. It will not be easy."

"Work, we can do." He hesitated, then accepting that she might have knowledge beyond his own, asked the question that preyed on everyone's mind. "Will we stay here? Or attempt to return?"

"There is no return to what we once had," she said sadly. "We can hope Aelynn has led us to our new home, and that we will be safe here."

Nautilus glanced up at the volcano and thought that highly unlikely, but for now, he kept his thoughts to himself. His missing crew came first.

He sent men to split fallen tree trunks and carry them toward the thicket of flowered shrubs the priestess chose for her temple.

* * *

While the men hacked at trees, Tasia sought the blessing of Aelynn in the tropical bower she'd selected. A sweet clear stream trickled over a pebble bed. Tall, heavily flowered bushes created a natural wall. The arching fronds of palms provided a ceiling.

It wasn't soaring marble and artistically carved and painted friezes, but she sensed the same peace here as in the lost sanctuary.

She kneeled and offered up prayers of thanksgiving for their safe passage. The spirit descended with more purity than it had at home. Her brow unfurrowed, her heart steadied, and she breathed deeply, wrapping herself in the bliss of acceptance.

In Tasia's inner vision, the goddess descended in a halo of light and clouds. With a sweep of her hand, Aelynn showed a future of fruitful gardens, a temple of flowers, sturdy homes...and children. *Be fruitful and multiply, raise your people in my name and by my precepts,* she commanded. *Understand me now...let the children be as children.*

Tasia drank in the serenity of the garden, the confidence that she'd never possessed, the future that could be theirs...

Daskala had to wake her from her trance. "Forgive my intrusion, my lady, but the altar is ready. The men are eager to leave and find their comrades. We would like to see Mageiras and Gaia and the others again."

Tasia rose, still awestruck by the power of the vision she'd been given. Had the fasting of these past days opened her mind? Or simply created hallucinations?

She blinked and realized it was dawn. She'd spent the night in Aelynn's temple.

"I am not certain if Aelynn or Aphrodite has lured us here," Tasia murmured, glancing around at the almost hedonistic surroundings, struggling to interpret the vision she'd received. "I believe Aelynn is demanding more worshippers. Our few numbers aren't sufficient."

Daskala's eyes widened. "You have Seen this? What does this mean? We are to convert the sailors?"

"That is one method," Tasia agreed dryly. "But she shows me children and tells us to be fruitful and multiply."

"How is that possible? Did not Aelynn command her vestals to be as children so she might speak to us?" Daskala asked in true puzzlement.

Tasia raised her eyebrows and waited for the older teacher to grasp what she herself did not entirely understand.

"Oh." Daskala looked pained, then warily interested. "Your vision cannot come from Aphrodite. Only Aelynn speaks through you. And she wants us to..." The teacher gestured helplessly, looking alarmed. "Then I suppose we must obey, somehow."

"I have seen you admiring the sailor called Demetri and think your agreement a little too convenient," Tasia said wryly. "But my vision says nothing of whether we might continue conversing with the goddess if we succumb to the pleasures of the flesh. I fear I am interpreting wrongly."

"In all my years, the goddess has never deigned to speak with me," Daskala said with a shrug. "I will assume I am not worthy. Before we resolve anything, we must find the others. It's the fate of all that we decide, and they must be part of the decision."

The pleasures of the flesh. Tasia shivered with the awareness of her surroundings and of the young, muscled men waiting on the beach. A priestess was chosen from those to whom the goddess spoke—and the goddess spoke only to virgins. Tasia had been receiving visions since infancy—the reason she'd been brought to the temple. Her family had thought her mad.

The women to whom the goddess had never spoken might be willing to give up their maidenhood and expectations, but a chosen priestess? That would take daring she did not possess. The goddess was her family.

Still... Gazing on the brawny captain shouting orders, waving muscled arms, standing in the sand like a human Zeus, Tasia yearned to feel the strength of his arms, the pounding of his heart, the sturdiness of his chest. Just once, if she could feel the pleasure of flesh against flesh, a gentle caress, a touch of fondness...

With regret, she turned away from any such knowledge and set her sights on preparing for the promised future. Her place was to bring Aelynn's dream of plenty to others.

Three

Nautilus and his crew kneeled outside the bower concealing the praying virgins. Their high, sweet voices stirred his blood as it shouldn't.

In all his years of duty in the service of the goddess, he had not once been tempted by the maidens in white hovering above him in their distant temple. He and his men had the freedom of the seas and shores, of lusty, colorful women who greeted them with welcoming arms. The vestals were ethereal angels not to be considered in such an earthly manner.

But days and nights on a narrow ship had proved the women were human. They hungered, they cried, they feared. And best of all, they had shapely legs and rounded curves.

If the goddess provided, and they found the other galley, the island would soon be housing nearly three dozen hungry men with almost an equal number of nubile virgins. Well, maybe somewhere around two dozen of each, if he didn't count the children.

Nautilus prayed his thanks that their mead supplies ran low.

"They have the voice of angels," Demetri, his first mate, declared with a transfixed expression. "Do you think we might be near friendly shores? Sicily is said to have beautiful women."

Nautilus followed the path of his thoughts easily enough since his own traveled the same direction. No man could remain sane resisting such lush bounty for long.

"First, we find our ship. Pray hard and divert your nasty thoughts," Nautilus admonished.

"You will have mutiny if you expect us to behave like eunuchs," Demetri protested. "This island is isolated as the other was not. We have nowhere to spend our coins."

"The goddess will provide," Nautilus said solemnly. After he'd watched the priestess bring his heathen men to their knees, perhaps he ought to start to believe, but he was a practical man, and the philosophy of worship didn't put food in his stomach. "It won't hurt you heathens to learn respect for goddesses and virgins."

Demetri slanted him a skeptical look but returned to praying.

Nautilus tuned in to the wind and the dawn sky and calculated the minutes until they could navigate the narrow passage back to the familiar sea.

The singing descended into a single chant accompanied by a rhythmic drum beat. A drum? Nautilus didn't remember instruments being brought aboard. Perhaps a hollow trunk.

The priestess emerged from beneath an arch of flowering vines. The white nimbus of her hair rippled over a newly cleaned tunic. The purple belt circled a narrow waist and emphasized the fullness of breast and hip. Power emanated from her presence.

As the dawn beamed upon her Venus-like beauty, his crew audibly gasped and bowed their heads, tearing their pagan gazes from her holiness.

Unbowed, Nautilus studied her without the veil of frantic urgency from these past days. Lady Tasia's skin was fine and lightly colored with pink from days in the wind, not bronzed like that of most of her handmaidens. She no longer looked so frail as earlier. The sea breeze molded her linen to a proud figure, a Venus worthy of worship.

Her speech distracted him from his musings.

"The goddess has spoken," she said in a clear voice that carried over the lapping of waves and the murmurs of men. "Our home is lost. She has brought us to a new one. The Chalice of Plenty will provide all we need. In this blessed garden, there will be water and food for all, a safe harbor for our ships, and peace. Our duty will be to protect the chalice from outsiders, and to this end, she has given us, her chosen people, many gifts. We are to use our gifts wisely for the betterment of all, and not just for ourselves. If we worship her and obey her laws, we—and our descendants—will be blessed forever. Go forth and sail with safety to find our friends and comrades."

She departed as silently as she had come, leaving the men gaping.

Their descendants?

Before speculation could run rampant, Nautilus was on his feet and heading for their remaining ship. "To sea, men! We must find our brothers." If anything, the lady had inspired his men to return here as quickly as they could.

If Nautilus prayed at all, he prayed that they'd find the other ship and return safely. If anything happened to both ships, the women would be left stranded and their goddess would have to provide men from Olympus.

* * *

"We have the pot the soldiers left for us," Daskala told Tasia. "We have the fire they started. We have water and fish to cook. But we need root vegetables as well as fruits to feed us. We need knives to clean the fish."

"The boys carry knives." Tasia pointed at one of the brown-eyed, brown-haired, half-naked youngsters the captain and his crew had left in their care. "Let them share in your duties. We must learn a whole new way of doing things, men and women together. We cannot survive apart in this world."

"Perhaps some of the boys could go with Sirene and look for roots?" Daskala asked tentatively.

"It would be better if we had Gaia to lead them, and Mageiras to look for spices," Tasia said sadly, speaking of the agronomist and the cook on the second ship.

She could not bear to consider the loss of so many valuable minds and hands. First, the task at hand. "Gaia would recognize plants similar to those we grew at home. Perhaps one of her acolytes has enough knowledge to help?"

"I will ask. If we are to stay here, we need Gaia's guidance in tilling our fields. We do not know what the winters will be like. How will we cook without herbs?" the teacher asked, muttering to herself as she walked away. The herbs had been stored on the second ship with the goats.

If plants were the only problem... Tasia began mental lists of tasks, most of which required tools and labor they did not have. Paradise had its limits.

Painfully aware that if the ships did not return, they would be abandoned forever despite the goddess's promise, Tasia kept a watch on the harbor and the sun. She knew it would not be possible for the men to return before dark, but the idea of spending the night here without adequate shelter or guardians worried her ceaselessly.

Should she have demanded they build a stronger lodging before they built the altar? Had she merely succumbed to hunger, and her vision of safety was just wishful dreaming?

To worsen her doubts, the day was not without its mishaps. One of the small boys twisted his ankle in an animal hole. While the younger girls screamed in fear that the hole might have been caused by snakes or worse, Tasia and Althaia wrapped the boy's limb in tree fronds and vines, and left him soaking it in a cool grotto pond.

Terrified of their poorly dug latrine, one of the smallest girls wept hysterically rather than use it. A very young carpenter's apprentice built her a bottomless stool to place over the hole, using his knife and vines and branches the other children gathered. It broke when the next child used it, starting another round of weeping.

By dark, Tasia wanted to cry from exhaustion, but everyone had been fed, the ill had been tended, and beds of moss had been prepared for all. She sat guard with Althaia, their Healer, for the first part of the evening, feeding their small fire and praying for the safe return of the ships.

But even she had to submit to sleep sometime.

By morning, the grumbling and fear had multiplied. The younger girls wept for their familiar meals and pets. The older women complained of aches and pains and glanced worriedly toward the harbor. Everyone griped about tramping through unfamiliar vegetation in search of food and fields and building material.

The pleasant, orderly routine of meals and classes and prayer had vanished with their home.

Then Khaos stumbled and spilled her bucket of water over their only cooking fire. Tempers snapped. Even Daskala screamed and ranted in desperation and anger. The nine-year-old Khaos wept heart-breakingly, sitting on the ground, hugging her knees, and rocking back and forth as if the world had ended.

Tasia picked the child out of the muddy ashes, brushed her off, and set her to attempting to make fire with kindling and their one flint. But nothing could be accomplished if tempers continued to flare.

"Sirene," Tasia begged at last. "Is there a song that might lighten their moods? Bring joy to the heart? We could all be at the bottom of the sea, feeding the fishes, or buried in debris had the goddess not saved us. We should spend our days in rejoicing."

Sirene obediently lifted her heavenly voice in a joyous hymn to the day, a simple hymn even the children knew. Within minutes, the clearing where they were constructing their shelters became a place of laughter. Happy shouts greeted the lifting of walls and completion of leaf roofs.

Tasia gazed upon the change in amazement. "It took only a song?" she asked Daskala, who was weaving palm fronds into a basket.

"And prayer, I'm sure," the elder teacher said soothingly. "Sirene's voice must reach the heavens."

Tasia did not remember Sirene's voice reaching the heavens on any other occasion, or their former priestess would have set the musician to singing day and night to prevent petty quarreling.

Khaos cried out her triumph as she produced fire in their small hearth, and those assigned to cooking hurried to set about their tasks with relief.

The worry over the missing ships seemed as endless and painful as the tasks they must accomplish. While Daskala muttered of the need for stronger shelter from storms, Tasia sent the youngest to splash in a pond and gather flowers for the altar.

"Play is worthless," Daskala argued. "We are alone now and must learn to work through the day. They are not too young to gather shellfish for our dinner."

"Would you break their spirits with endless work?" Tasia asked, sitting down to join her teacher in weaving the fronds. "Children learn from play. The goddess has promised us plenty. We are not hungry. One day at a time is all we can hope to take."

"Do you mean we can never leave this place for civilization?" the teacher protested in anguish. "I have no purpose here. My scrolls are useless when all we do is work. The young will grow up ignorant."

"Of course we can leave, just as we could leave the temple if we chose to give up that life. I would miss you, if you chose to go, but I wish you would stay so that we could learn this new life together. We must thank Khaos for bringing the scrolls." Tasia's hands trembled with weariness and her heart sobbed with sorrow, but as leader, she could not let others see her doubt and pain. Someone had to be strong.

"We will die here," the older woman said with a sigh.

"We will die anywhere," Tasia responded with amusement. "We

escaped dying in the quake and again in the storm. I do not think Aelynn has brought us here to die of hunger."

But they might die of loneliness and grief if the ships did not return.

They'd scarcely acknowledged the existence of the soldiers until the quake had rearranged their lives. And now, it was difficult not to think of them—and of their missing sisters.

At dusk, without permission or even a means of doing so, Khaos set fire to a stack of dry seaweed on the high cliff overlooking the harbor.

* * *

Eyelids drooping with weariness, Nautilus stood high in the bow of his ship in the last minutes before dawn, urging his equally exhausted men to row. Lashed to the rear was their foundering sister ship.

"We don't have enough strength to pull both boats," Styros argued. "Let's take our losses before we lose this one."

"When will we have the materials, tools, and boatbuilders to build another?" Nautilus asked. "We don't know what the future holds. We can't afford to waste anything. Now that we have everyone safely aboard, we've doubled our crew. Let half a dozen men rest for a few hours, then send another half dozen below. We'll manage."

"The gods be praised that we found them," Styros said. "But besides killing the men with exhaustion, we need to make better time. We're out of fresh water. There is illness among the women. One of the lads may lose his foot from that blow he took in the storm. People are more important than ships."

"You are like a demon nagging on my shoulder," Nautilus complained. "Go rest. We've accomplished the impossible already these past days. We'll hope we can prove our worthiness to the goddess."

Styros snorted. "They have you believing in such things? You've gone weak in the head." He gestured at the foggy night sky. "We have no stars to guide us back to those rocks."

"I'm willing to believe that the priestess saved us. That's enough for me." Nautilus wasn't entirely certain he believed his own words, but if he said them with confidence, he might make Styros believe.

At least the man stomped off to rest, leaving the captain to await the dawn alone.

Nautilus prayed that the lady was holding her own without aid from any but a few handmaidens and boys. Surely they would not starve in a few days.

Except—*An entire island had disappeared into the sea in a few minutes.* And their new home seemed determined to vanish into the mists just as certainly as the sea had claimed the old—once more, heavy fog blanketed the ship.

Perhaps he really ought to pray to the goddess. Without the navigation of the stars, they had no guarantee they would ever find their new home again.

The fog swirled around the masts, and the wind abandoned the sails—just as before. A few groans from below gave evidence that the rowers were weary enough to notice.

For all Nautilus knew, in this miasma he'd been robbed of his senses and was sailing into a dream. He had no vision of rock cliffs to guide him, just the instincts that he'd started to doubt.

A tall, brown-skinned handmaiden strode up to stand beside him, admiring the horizon. "The goddess awaits," she murmured in awe. "See how the sun shines like gold from the heavens on our new home."

He blinked, and damned if it didn't. He knew sailors often saw illusions in the waters, but this was in the air. It was as if the rocks produced a miasma to conceal the sun. But if one knew the fog was an illusion and looked above, he could see the dawn's light transforming the sky into a golden mist shimmering with rainbows, illuminating the rocks surrounding the island, inviting them to land.

Or to crash upon the rocky barrier.

How had the woman—perhaps all the women—seen what he had not? That served as reminder that the goddess's acolytes were chosen for their special abilities. If seeing sun where there was none was one of them, perhaps they had others.

"Can any of your women help the rowers?" he asked the maiden who had so mysteriously seen the island before he did.

"If they will let us." Without another word, she departed on her errand, disappearing as swiftly as she had appeared.

He would have to learn her name—and those of all the women—if they were to combine forces as the Priestess had said.

There was only one way of joining forces with women that he knew, but he would gratefully learn all their names for that reason alone. Had the priestess truly said they would have *descendants*? Had the goddess lifted the boundaries around her maidens?

His entire attitude would shift—if he believed in the Elysian Fields here on earth. But such a garden of the gods did not exist. He would have to return to Greece and hope to put his future back together again some other way. A man without wife and family was nothing.

The two ships limped through the thick fog. Nautilus navigated by his instincts, testing the currents and winds in search of the narrow aperture that would return them to paradise. These cliffs would present a formidable fortress against weather and mankind. Perhaps a sentinel on the highest rock with a signal...

A golden light caught his armbands, and the fog parted sufficiently to see the craggy crevasse the priestess had insisted they sail. On his own, he would never have taken such a risk. Leave it to one who knew nothing to discover new worlds!

Dreaming of alluring sylph-like curves and hair finer than silk, Nautilus startled abruptly back to the moment with a shout from the rigging.

Glancing up, he watched in horror at the fire spreading across the island bluffs.

Fire, not the sun, had illuminated the thick fog.

Chapter Four

Tasia saw the flames ignite on the bluff and immediately raced in that direction. She was fairly certain that was Khaos up there, playing with her new-found ability to start fire.

As the wind caught the sparks, the fire spread through the dry grass. Khaos sprinted down the hill with flames licking at her heels.

The fire was outracing the girl's short legs. She'd be engulfed in flames in seconds. Tasia grabbed a bucket of water one of the girls had filled and shouted at the horror-struck vestals. "Save the scrolls and the chalice. Follow Daskala."

"To the harbor!" Daskala shouted. "Hold the scrolls above your heads! Into the water."

Tasia was already on her way up the hill, running toward the spreading flames as her vestals ran in the opposite direction.

She heard the others screaming at her to turn back, but the little girl's cries of pain couldn't be ignored. Just as it had at home, instinct or Aelynn guided her—not fear or thought.

She caught Khaos just as the fire engulfed her. Splashing water on the closest flames, Tasia pushed the child to the ground and fell on top of her. Together, they rolled in the dirt through the flames— and off the grassy verge into the darkness below.

* * *

A brisk breeze caught the galley's sail once they reached the open harbor, but Nautilus focused on the growing flames on the bluff, not the beach where the women raced into the water.

With a horror so gut deep that he nearly fell to his knees, he watched the priestess and the child go up in flames and disappear through the smoke.

If they had fallen from the cliffs, they would have met certain death in the water, but he hadn't heard the splash or seen them fall. Perhaps they'd rolled down the hill. Or lay dead upon the burned grass. The gods may as well have ripped the heart from his chest.

His rowers could not row fast enough. The breeze was not

strong enough, and it carried them toward the main beach, not the more northern bluff. Nautilus ran to the bow and without further thought, dived into the water.

The fiery point where child and lady met was emblazoned across his mind so clearly he might never see the stars again.

He reached the narrow top half of the crescent harbor and climbed the rocks toward the fiery grass above. The scent of scorched earth and smoke filled his nose, but praise Aelynn, not the scent of burned flesh.

Exhausted from the swim and the rapid climb to the top of the cliff, he dropped to the blackened grass, singeing his soaked tunic. He gasped for breath, and oriented himself. Where were the priestess and the child?

Flames licked down the hill, catching at shrubs and dry grasses. The rocky slope prevented the flames from jumping quickly or higher.

He had to be in the right place, but he saw no priestess, heard no cries except those of the circling birds.

The hot rocks blistered his hands and the soles of his feet as he pushed himself up. Had Aelynn swept the priestess to her bosom in a cloud of glory?

Nautilus would rather believe that than imagine her silver-blond halo burned beyond recognition. Despite his vague notion of Elysian Fields for the holy, his practical nature dragged him onward to trudge across the hot earth, crying, "Lady Tasia!" in accompaniment to the mournful cries of seabirds.

Below, his crew beached the galleys. They knew how to douse fire. The women would be safe in the water. It was the priestess who mattered.

What would become of these people without the lady? He'd had hopes of sailing back to Greece once the women were safe, but they would be helpless without their priestess.

He'd lost much in his life, but this was a loss he didn't think any of them could surmount. In a few short days, the fair lady had become indispensable—even to him.

Fear pounding through his blood, Nautilus scrambled down an old rock slide. Loose gravel gave away beneath his feet, and he slid into a ravine untouched by flame. The damned island was a treacherous trap.

He winced as his ribs cracked against a boulder, halting his rapid descent. "Lady Tasia!"

This time, he thought he heard a weak cry. Praising whatever gods watched over them, he worked his way deeper into the ravine on his rear, rather than risk breaking bones.

Even if she were close, how could she have survived the tumble without breaking frail limbs? And the fire! He'd seen them enveloped in flame.

"Here, Lord Captain," a child's voice cried. "I can hear you. We're down here!"

Not knowing whether to expire of relief or dread, Nautilus crawled among the tumbled rocks, searching for whatever hole hid his goal. Why was the priestess not calling to him too?

The rocks were cooler here, bypassed by the flames for lack of vegetation. Black gravel and small stones slithered beneath his weight, and he feared causing a cascade upon the pair he sought.

"Have you a stick or cloth you can wave so I can see you?" he called.

"The hole is too high above me," the child replied. "It's dark down here."

A cave beneath the earth, perhaps, although how they'd ended there, he couldn't tell. Belly down, he crawled in circles, searching for a fissure that would show him anything but stone or reveal a glimpse of white. "Move about, child. Perhaps I can see you then."

"I can't," the plaintive voice cried. "I hurt too much."

Where was the priestess?

May Mars and Poseidon in Olympus take note and help him find the beauty he had lost and rescue that poor child. Cursing his sinful ways, recognizing that he had no right to expect the aid of gods, Nautilus began moving boulders, pushing them down the slope, away from the voice and into the rocky wash below. "Can you still hear me, child?"

"Yes," she said eagerly, if weakly. "And I can see your hand in the hole you've opened."

His *hand*. How would he climb through a hole a hand span wide? How had they ended up where no man could go?

Finding an opening that might be the hole she saw, he gripped the boulder covering it and pushed. A larger hole in the rocky spill appeared.

"Thank you, Lord Captain," the child whispered. "I can see light."

She was shattering what remained of his wicked hard heart.

Once the larger boulders were removed, he could see that the hole he had uncovered was more of a cleft in the side of the hill. By all Hades, how had they ended up there? He pushed aside a tall stone that blocked his shoulders and slid in sideways, then dropped to the floor.

The removal of another few large stones would allow him to walk out, he calculated. Gazing up, he could see the first stone he removed had essentially been in the ceiling.

He gazed around the poorly lit space. "Where are you child? Where is Lady Tasia?"

Deeper into the cavern, the girl waved a blackened, tattered tunic that appeared to cover her arm. "I am here. The lady is looking for a way out."

The lady was still alive! Nautilus fell to his knees in an uncharacteristic gesture and offered up gratitude to a deity he hadn't believed in. Whoever or whatever had saved the child and the priestess deserved thanks. It could be the volcano for all he cared.

He crept closer to the white rag, trying to hide his horror at the sight of the child in little or nothing. The fire had burned away most of her clothing. Soot and ash blackened much of her skin. Was it a blessing that she even lived?

"Do you know which way the lady went?" he asked, concealing his dismay.

She pointed to a darker shadow along the wall.

To his surprise, Nautilus could stand inside the cavern. He had no light other than the entrance, but the ceiling appeared to be high. He glanced around and located the hole far above him that they must have fallen through. Neither the child nor the priestess would have been able to climb back out.

"She has no doubt gone for help," he told the girl, stripping off his wet chiton to cover her. "If you begin to fear we're lost, wave this out that opening." He pointed at the way he'd entered, praying she would be able to reach it, fearful of moving her without aid.

She clutched the wool with a hand that gleamed white enough to be whole, thank all the gods.

He probed a darker shadow on the wall that he had assumed

was an opening. It was too dark to see any barrier, but his hand met with a strange resistance, almost like a wall of pine resin. He couldn't feel rock, but it was as if a thick bubble protected the fissure. He applied his shoulder and pushed through anyway. No resin stuck to him. He broke through to normal air on the other side.

Once past the odd barrier, he stood in a large cavern strangely lit with phosphorescence along the walls. Was this some sort of mystical place?

He saw no sign of the priestess.

Hurrying across the rocky floor to another shadowy crevasse, he again encountered the bubble-air. This time, when he broke through, he found the priestess wearily slumped upon the floor. Only the fact that she sat up kept his heart from collapsing with her.

"There is no way out," she said mournfully. "Are you an apparition?"

"You look like one more than I do," he replied, trying for calm but not certain he'd achieved it.

From what little he could see, her tunic was burned to tatters, but enough fabric remained to cling to her shoulders. He couldn't tell if soot, dirt, or burns marred her arms. She held her elbow and cradled one arm against her chest.

"The others?" she asked in what seemed to be weary resignation. "If you are not an apparition, does this mean everyone is safe?"

"As safe as we are," he agreed. "And I am no apparition."

"Then how did you get in?" She gazed at his hand in weary wonder but didn't take it. She stood on her own, still clutching her arm. "You are much too large for any hole I found."

"Brute force works better than prayers most times." Assuming she'd hurt her left arm, he steadied her with a hand to her right elbow. "There's a good-sized entrance once I removed a few boulders. What is this spongy stuff we're walking through?" He shoved through first, letting her follow behind him.

"I'm not certain. It feels...protective. It's as if the earth opened up and took us in and would like us to stay. But Khaos needs our Healer, and I couldn't carry her."

As they entered the smaller cavern with its sliver of light, Nautilus studied the way the lady held one arm tightly wrapped inside her tunic. Had she broken it? It pained him to think of her hurting. He wanted to help, but he couldn't mend broken bones. He needed to find some way of taking them both to their healer.

"How do I lift the child?" he murmured helplessly when they reached the girl and discovered her unconscious. He could throw a grown man over his shoulder—but a small child, burned and hurting—was beyond him.

"Her name is Khaos. She's a perennial troublemaker, but not out of meanness." The lady kneeled beside her student and touched her throat. "She lives and breathes. If you could slide your chiton under her, perhaps we could make a bundle in which to carry her?"

Holding his breath, Nautilus gently lifted the child, who moaned but did not wake while the priestess slid the cloth beneath her. Once he laid her on the wool, they bundled up the corners, and he carried her gently, trying not to let anything touch her but the wet wool of his mantle.

He had no other hand to aid the lady as they climbed out the rocky entrance. She continued holding her arm to her chest but made no complaint, simply gasping in relief at emerging beneath the sky again.

"How could you possibly find us?" she asked in wonder as she gazed down the burned bluff to the ships in the harbor. "I cannot even imagine how you found the other galley in all that vast sea."

"Knowledge, experience, stubbornness," he declared, looking for an easy path so she wouldn't fall and hurt herself worse. "Nothing supernatural, I'm sure."

She laughed in a low, melodic voice. "The arrogance of a man who believes he is capable of great feats without help from above. Who, then, will make the laws on this new land, the goddess or arrogant men?"

"Men will, as always." He wished to touch her, to hold her elbow as they walked the difficult path, but the weight of the child took both hands. Talk was his only means of reaching out to her. "Should we choose to stay here, we'll have a council, just as at home. But do not fear, we respect you and your maidens. We will see that you have your temple and your studies, just as before, if this is where you decide to stay. But first there is the matter of returning to see if all we knew is lost."

"Very well, we will start there," she said, as they slipped and slid on the gravel. "Aelynn has never sought worshippers. They have

simply come to us as word of her greatness spread, but in this time
of war, men do not seek peace. I do not know Her reasoning in
isolating us here. I suppose you must return to our island and see if
we can go back. Perhaps this is only meant to be a temporary
haven."

She did not sound in the least convinced but seemed to be
humoring him. She winced and grabbed her arm tighter as she
stumbled at the bottom. Nautilus feared a priestess was stoic but not
immune to pain.

Standing on the slope above the natural harbor, Nautilus
contemplated the serene island spread out as far as the eye could
see, and the people watching them from the shore. "We must at least
offer the choice of staying or returning," he agreed. "This is a lonely
place, and some of my men have families."

"My women do not," she whispered in regret, straightening and
adjusting her arm to a more comfortable position. "Their families
sacrificed them to the goddess. There is no home for them
elsewhere."

"They can never marry?" he asked with curiosity, hoping he was
distracting her from her pain as they clambered down the last of the
rocks. He saw no sign of animal paths anywhere.

"It happens occasionally, but we lose any hope of communing
with the goddess if we choose an earthly fate."

Her noncommittal tone and phrasing told Nautilus that she had
a very distinct opinion about marrying off her maidens but refrained
from expressing it. If they must work together, as it was becoming
increasingly apparent that they must, he needed to understand her
better.

"You do not approve of marriage," he stated. "Why?"

She hesitated. They had almost reached the beach. The fire
seemed to have been quenched. Women were rushing toward them.
She nodded in their direction. "Each of my vestals is a strong,
capable woman with talents they have been allowed to develop in
service of the goddess. They do not need a man's strength except to
save them from other men. What will become of them and their
abilities as some man's possession?"

Two tall comely virgins met them with open arms, reaching for
the bundle he held. Nautilus surrendered the unconscious child and
watched her easily carted off by the women. In this, the priestess

was right. His masculine strength and experience was not needed to tend a child.

As people surrounded them, he could not respond to the lady's argument, but he knew the answer—at home, these competent women would have been used for child-bearing and cooking and ignored for all other purposes.

He was fairly certain the priestess was telling him that wouldn't happen here.

Chapter Five

"We're taking Khaos to the grotto pool," Althaia said, not hiding her horror at the child's condition.

Following in the Healer's path, Tasia hid her pain and turned to Nautilus. "This is Althaia's dominion. You must return to reassure the others that all is being done that can be. Perhaps your men can help prepare a meal?"

"They can do that and more, my lady," the captain said with alacrity.

She had seen and felt the strength of his hands, benefitted from his brave heroism, but it was the concern in his eyes that warmed her frozen heart. Still, despite her pain, Tasia shook her head at him, denying his need to do more.

"I will be fine in Althaia's hands, if I know the others are well."

His anxious gaze studied her expression and noted her arm, but he blessedly did not argue. With a reluctant nod, he loped off down a path already beaten through the jungle of foliage.

"I have only the herbs in my bag. We must search for more," Althaia said, once Nautilus was out of sight.

"How are those who just arrived on the ships?" Tasia asked, concealing her pain and keeping her voice low. "Is Gaia well enough to go out with her assistant to look for herbs?"

"They're exhausted and dehydrated." Althaia eyed Tasia's arm as they hurried after the women carrying Khaos. "But water here is plentiful. They can fill flasks to take with them on their search."

"This will not be an easy life if we stay here." Tasia translated her Healer's fear. She would have Khaos looked at first before admitting her own agony. "We have always had the mainland to call on before."

"I admit, I had hoped we could return to the temple. Some of my herbs are very rare. I came away with only a few seeds that I'd brought for blessing, and we may not be able to grow them here."

They arrived at the grotto containing the spring-fed bathing pool. Althaia instructed the others in removing the tatters from the patient's burns. She pointed wordlessly at a rock ledge for Tasia.

Unable to do more than hold her broken limb while everyone labored over Khaos, Tasia obeyed the unspoken order. She was so exhausted, she could sleep upright. She closed her eyes and leaned against the mossy wall.

She would have to send a ship out to let those people go who would not accept living here. They must see for themselves that their home was destroyed and decide their own fates.

Would this displease Aelynn? She did not know. Perhaps she should fast again to see if the goddess would speak to her.

She must have slept. When Althaia woke her, torches lit the grotto, and only one vestal remained to support Khaos in the water. Charis waited with her basket of fresh garments.

"Bathe first," Althaia ordered. "Then I will bind that arm."

"Khaos?" Tasia asked anxiously.

"She is actually sleeping. The water soothes her pain. I have used my salve on those burns above the water. I have no more, so the water must protect her."

"Anything that keeps the child still is welcome," Tasia said with a smile, followed by a groan as she attempted to remove her charred tunic.

"I looked while you slept. The bone doesn't seem to have broken through your skin. Just step into the pool with your clothes on. We'll work off the fabric."

Tasia hesitated. "Are we dirtying the drinking water?"

"We've been testing this spring. It has a different source than that of the ones we use for drinking and seems to flow directly to the harbor." Althaia helped her to find a seat on a low ledge inside the pool. "Charis brought your soaps. She must have gathered half your belongings while the rest of us ran for safety. Here, let me see that arm."

"Charis is a gift from the goddess," Tasia acknowledged, smiling at her maidservant.

The water lapped around her, easing aching muscles. By the time she bathed with her maid's help, she was nearly asleep again. When Althaia set and splinted the bone, the pain abruptly woke her. By that time, her arm was nearly wrapped, and she felt miraculously well—and starved. With aid, she was able to climb out of the bath and don fresh clothing. Then Althaia braced Tasia's arm against her chest in a length of linen.

"The men are cooking fish over fires on the beach," Charis said, wrapping up the rest of the contents of the basket she'd carried to the grotto. "We've gathered oranges and lemons, and Gaia has approved several plant leaves for wrapping until we can bake bread. They're quite tasty when roasted. Shall you rest here and let me bring some to you?"

"No, I need to join the others, let them see that I am fine." And verify with her own eyes that the people in her charge fared well. "Did the fire cause much damage?"

Amazed that her arm did not throb, Tasia stepped cautiously from the bathing cavern, not wishing to jar her broken bone with a misstep.

"The men put out the fire before it reached our camp. They are posting guards now, working on the ships, manly things," Charis said with a shrug of her square shoulders.

"I trust they at least let the little ones sleep," Tasia said wryly as they traversed a path already well worn by many feet.

"They do whatever it is they have always done. Perhaps routine reassures."

"Very astute. Routine will be difficult, but we can aim for it. Soft beds and plentiful food will be a good start."

"The men require wine," Charis said cheerfully. "That one's a little more difficult since we filled the barrels mostly with water."

A problem for another day. Tasia had hoped to slip quietly into the clearing where her people congregated, but the captain had sharp eyes. His tall golden form unfolded from a rock to stand at attention the moment she left the shelter of the trees.

Following the captain's gaze, his men also rose to their feet. And because they did, so did the women. Sirene broke out in song.

Embarrassed, uncertain how to handle such unwarranted attention, Tasia tried to gesture for them to sit, but her arm was bound tightly to her chest and one hand didn't create an effective gesture.

"Please, honor the goddess who brought us to safety and not her humble priestess. It is good to see all of you together again. We have missed you. We'll need to say prayers of gratitude for your safe return, but for now, sit, eat. In the morning, perhaps, we must make decisions." Tasia settled on a rock far from the bonfire and let them do the same.

As they ate, the men told seafaring stories that held her maidens enthralled. The days aboard ship had eased some of their fears of the rough sailors. Tasia knew more hurdles waited ahead, but for now, she enjoyed the tranquility.

"Your arm?" The captain asked, coming to kneel on the sand beside her. "And the child?"

"Both are doing well, thanks to your quick thinking—and swimming, I hear."

"I won't always be here," he pointed out carefully. "Until we've explored this land, we must keep the children in one place."

Tasia sighed and sipped the juice that Charis handed her. It tasted of ambrosia, or how she imagined ambrosia must taste. Not until she'd finished her first leaf-wrapped fish did she reply.

"There are nearly two dozen children under the age of twelve. War and famine have caused many families to sacrifice their daughters of late. And apparently you have taken in many young apprentices for the same reason."

He bowed his head in acknowledgment. "Once, a lad had to have a dozen years before he was brought to us. These times, they beg us to take their youngest in hopes they'll be fed and cared for while they learn a trade that will provide in years to come."

"This island is far, far larger than our previous home. There, we knew they could find little trouble without discovery. Here, it is impossible. We cannot tie them to trees."

"And everyone is busy with chores, I understand." He sat beside her, holding a plate of chopped fruits that Charis brought for him.

"Perhaps we should compile an agenda to discuss in the morning. I have never attended a council. Are there rules we should establish?"

"Councils don't include women," he reminded her.

He said that while wearing a twinkle in his eye. She didn't hesitate to rise to the bait. "Then that is the first rule we will change."

He apparently saved argument for the morning. For now, they settled in companionable silence while the women sang and the sailing stories grew bolder.

"It will not be so easy to keep my men from your women as they become more familiar," Nautilus warned as the night waned and the children were taken to their separate shelters by their elders.

"The goddess has acknowledged that," Tasia told him. "But I am too weary to understand how we change things. If some of my maidens decide they prefer earthly pleasures to godly ones, there must be some order, some ceremony, some recognition similar to marriage."

"Not as easy as it sounds, my lady," he warned. "You have not been raised in the world and do not understand the nature of men."

"I'll admit, I do not. And I assume your men do not understand the nature of my women. The children brought to us are the special ones, the ones blessed—or cursed—by the gods. I am their spiritual leader, but not a governing one. Our decisions are made by the eldest among us."

"As my officers rule over the less experienced. Perhaps, if this must be our new life, the women can continue governing domestic affairs, while my officers deal with finding safe harbors for trade and protection as before. But we should not discuss this while you're weary. Let us separate the idlers tonight and start fresh in the morning."

A few of the younger man and women were reluctant to part from the fire and the company, but the habit of obedience won for the moment. Tasia knew that could not last, but difficulties always seemed more insurmountable at night.

In the morning, surely they would see solutions to the very human dilemmas ahead of them.

Chapter 6

Nautilus admired the work accomplished within a week—and the priestess currently giving thanks for it. So far, they had avoided the disruptive need for discussing laws in favor of tackling tasks that needed to be accomplished first.

While the others chanted and prayed in their daily ceremony, Nautilus turned his attention from admiring the lady's beauty to the altar she stood in front of. Oddly, the hasty creation seemed to have grown to fit the bower.

The four stumps of trees from which they had carved the altar planks served as pedestals. The women had set their sacred chalice and bouquets of flowers on the high planks held by the pedestals. The stumps had begun to spring back to life with green sprouts and pink flowers. A mossy cover now enveloped the planks in a velvety emerald. If he believed in such things, Nautilus would call the altar—and perhaps the island—enchanted.

The priestess was another reason for amazement. Already, she'd removed the linen imprisoning her broken arm and seemed able to move it without pain. She held the chalice carefully, lifting it just enough for her acolytes to take a sip of whatever concoction they used for their ceremony.

Impatient for the council meeting they'd finally scheduled, he studied the hardened sailors and soldiers around him. They were all—men and boys alike—half infatuated with the fair priestess. They sat spell-bound, listening to her pray for wisdom, not grasping the lady's underlying message.

"May Aelynn bless us with this land," she recited as if in prayer, "and give us voices in our futures. We pray that we may be provided with the wisdom to seek the betterment of all. May she grant us the power to succeed at our chosen tasks."

"Does that mean I could choose farming instead of fishing?" young Georgós asked with interest.

Nautilus hid his smile at the lady's manipulative oration. In between the words of her prayers, she promised equality, fairness, and justice for all. Heady promises to people who expected a lifetime of servitude, even for his men, who didn't realize she also meant for women. She'd almost convinced the younger crew that happiness began with listening to women.

Nautilus pondered the possibility of sailing away to bring back women less inclined to preach and hold themselves on virtuous pedestals. The notion made his shoulders twitch—he wasn't prepared to pollute this perfect place just yet. He liked these knowledgeable women.

Instead, he was stupidly holding out hope that the priestess would repeat her promise of *descendants*. Once upon a time, he'd expected to raise strong sons to support him when he grew old and frail. He'd even negotiated with a merchant for marriage to his daughter to provide those sons. That time seemed distant now. A black-haired beauty could not compete with this vibrant priestess holding an entire population in thrall.

Marrying for wealth and position no longer held the same appeal as marrying a woman who was his match in wits. After spending the past days working in the company of these women, he'd realized just how different each one was. Women weren't as interchangeable as he'd thought. Now he wanted a woman of his own choice, one with the strength and intelligence to survive and protect his children when the earth quaked and mountains crumbled.

If he could, he would choose the intriguing priestess. A woman like that would make a good sailor's wife—strong, independent...

But not available for slaking his lust or providing sons.

"You have chosen your council leaders," the lady said, after setting aside the chalice. "If you will follow those leaders to the clearing set aside for our meeting, we will discuss our futures."

The children, led by their younger teachers, raced for the freedom of the harbor and the beach. Only their elders solemnly proceeded toward the meeting, each with their own concerns.

Nautilus maneuvered his way to Lady Tasia's side. "Shall I escort you, my lady? Your arm seems to have healed remarkably well. Is there no pain?" He boldly took her good elbow and led her down the path without waiting for permission. He reveled in her closeness, in the exotic flowery scent that seemed to be hers alone, in the sway of her hip brushing next to his. That she did not object swelled him with pride.

Except that she did not appear to notice his proprietary gesture much less object to it.

"I know you do not believe, Captain, but Aelynn seems to have given us an enchanted isle. Althaia is a good Healer, but even Khaos is recovering with amazing swiftness. Perhaps there is something in the water?" Big sea-blue eyes lifted to him as if he might actually know the answer.

"I thought the same thing, I'm afraid to admit," he acknowledged. "I have never heard of water that heals, if that is what you're asking. But I have only sailed this sea, and not the oceans beyond."

"That's far more experience than I possess," she said, looking pleased that he'd understood her reason for asking him. "I am aware that we tend to apply superstitious reasoning to that which we cannot explain. I don't wish to seem foolish if there are rational explanations."

"I prefer to accept what can't be explained and use it to my benefit when I can. You fooled no one with your oratory," he told her with a smile. "Despite your lovely promises, women do not belong on councils. They are too emotional and irrational."

"There speaks the ungodly male," she replied in equal amusement. "I like that you are intelligent and honest. But you are also wrong. You need to start accepting what cannot be changed."

"So must you, my lady. Women may pray and heal, but men will not be led by them." Nautilus offered her a bench at the front of the clearing where the other chosen leaders gathered. Two more of the women came to stand beside the priestess—Gaia, the one who had seen the fire on the island before him, and Althaia, the Healer. Nautilus had learned that the tall, bronzed Gaia was a gardener, and the Healer was a sturdy lass with thick silken black tresses and an almost Asiatic appearance.

His men had chosen Styros and Demetri, along with their captain, to lead the discussion. Accustomed to command, Nautilus took his place in front of the others, gesturing for everyone to be seated and quiet.

* * *

Behind the domineering captain, Tasia smiled reassurance at

her acolytes in the audience. Her women knew how to plan and
debate among themselves. Uneasy at allowing common sailors into a
discussion of their futures, they had gathered to one side of the
clearing. The nights of sharing a meal had been pleasant, but not
quite as momentous as deciding their fate.

Tasia sat quietly while the male council leaders lined up their
agenda for exploration, returning to seek families and former
homes, providing for those who remained here. These were
important decisions, and the men knew the sea better than she did.
That might change with time. The goddess seldom saw fit to show
the distant future. Aelynn preferred to deal with more immediate
needs and dangers.

When the men seemed intent on occupying the floor, Tasia
gestured for Gaia and Althaia to step up. The captain politely
brought his men into order. He stepped aside to let the ladies
explain what they needed to begin farming the land for food, finding
healing herbs, and teaching the children. The men instantly began to
argue over the necessity of teaching the boys to sail versus
classrooms.

As the clamor became more vociferous, Tasia pushed in front of
Nautilus, who roared for quiet. She raised her hands, and out of
respect, her women silenced. The sailors followed suit.

"We *must* change to survive," she reminded them. "We no
longer have our warm buildings, our access to larger markets. There
are those of you with families who wish to go home. Others would
like to return to the way things used to be, but that is not possible.
Even those who go home will find that life has changed unbearably.
But Aelynn has spoken. Only those who worship her will be allowed
to return to the island."

She sensed Nautilus's jerk of surprise, but she did not release
her audience by turning to him. "We cannot do everything at once.
We cannot make every decision now. Food and shelter come first.
Those who wish to return home should join the first exploratory
venture. And that means women as well as men," she warned.

"And in fairness," she continued, "those men who no longer
wish to sail the seas should be allowed to stay here and help us build
a new community."

Tasia was no fool. She knew the question uppermost among the
minds of men, the question she and her women had carefully

discussed among themselves these past days since Tasia had translated the goddess's desire differently than Alexandria had.

The virgin life had been chosen for them by their families. Some of her maidens preferred it that way. Others were of a more earthy nature. All of them were curious and terrified. She did not know how to address the question.

"There are so very few of us," she continued cautiously, "we must each do our parts and more, so it's best to do what we enjoy most. I see no reason why men can't farm and women can't fish. We will help and teach each other."

Tasia was not surprised when Nautilus gently elbowed her aside.

"We do not have separate shelters and villages as before," he reminded her. "If we are to be a community that lives together, then my men need wives. Will the goddess provide?"

Tasia fought the amused twitch of her lips at the bold way he stated the question she hadn't dared address. All the men sat up straighter, and Nautilus met her gaze defiantly. She knew little of men, but she was learning.

"Yes, I believe marriage is Aelynn's intention, for those who so choose. I fear this means the number of potential priestesses will dwindle while we build this new world, but surely Aelynn has taken that into consideration. In the future, perhaps the numbers of vestals will increase again. But for now, Aelynn is most clear. She wants her worshippers to be fruitful and multiply. She has not provided instructions."

Now, her women were clinging to her every word. She was about to release them from time-honored vows they had taken when they were too young to know what chastity meant. They had been as children then. Aelynn had said they need not be as children now.

"My ladies are very special in many ways," Tasia continued, "but none of us are experienced. This is another project that cannot be accomplished overnight. So all of you must consider how best we should establish courtship and permanent unions. *Permanent*," she insisted. "As in life-long commitment in order to raise new children and vestals in Aelynn's name."

Among the silent and stunned audience, only Charis raised her hand. Tasia nodded for her trusted maid to speak.

"There are nearly two dozen orphans under the age of twelve

who deserve families of their own. If some of us..." she hesitated, unused to speaking in public. "If some of us choose to live without men, could we commit to other women in order to raise the orphans?"

Interesting notion. Tasia heard titters among the crowd that indicated Charis had either asked the question wrong or meant something Tasia did not understand. Her inexperience was a liability, but still, she saw no harm. Aelynn had not specified *how* children must be taught.

"I don't see why not," Tasia told Charis. "Aelynn's women have raised children through the ages as a group. This must change if we are to make room for men and bring more children into the world. Those of you who do not wish to commit to a man must decide for yourselves whether you wish to take orders pledging your lives to the goddess and remain unpaired as we have in the past, or if you'd prefer a more worldly partnership with another woman to help with the rearing of orphans. In either case, the goddess expects you to follow her precepts as always. We are still Aelynn's children, and we worship her as always by living as she directs."

Nautilus poked her in the side, and she realized a few of the men were still watching her in expectation. She floundered a moment until she applied her knowledge of her ladies to rough soldiers. Her eyes widened in surprise, but she nodded acknowledgment.

"And of course, the same goes for the men. You have lived among yourselves for most of your lives. You may already have partners. We probably ought to find some way of formalizing all relationships so the rest of the community recognizes our choices. We must do what is best for the children, because they are our future, the ones who will care for us when we no longer can."

"Women committed to a goddess won't give us sons," one of the council leaders objected.

Tasia smiled gently at him. "Then perhaps you need to convince some good woman that she would rather commit to you, Styros. Although if you go outside this island, then you must find a woman who will not only give up her home, but whatever gods she worships. Perhaps you could learn to be very charming."

The men laughed. It was apparent that charm was not one of the sailor's attributes.

On this note, Nautilus brought the meeting to an end. Before Tasia could escape for a moment of peaceful prayer, the captain grabbed her good elbow and steered her from the excited chatter following the meeting.

"We are the leaders here," he reminded her. "We should show the others how it is best to establish courtships and commitments. There is no other man on this island better prepared to be your equal than I am."

Admittedly, she'd dared think the same, but his bold acknowledgment stunned her. His bare hand on her flesh tingled in an enticing manner that she very much desired to explore. The part of her that longed to be a woman preened knowing that a brave, strong leader of men had chosen her above all others. The part of her that had studied human behavior since childhood laughed and approved his aggressive approach.

Her too-human heart was annoyed that he did not express desire or affection but only the practicality of leadership.

The core of her that was committed to the goddess shook her head in sorrow. "You do not understand," she said sadly. "The goddess only speaks to a chosen few. We live our lives in chastity hoping to be among the chosen. If one of us forsakes her vows, then she forsakes any chance of receiving Aelynn's visions. At the moment, we have no other Seer among us besides me, unless one of the children manifests such an ability. And even then, it will be years of training before she can take the position of priestess. If all my women choose to give up their chastity, there is only me to receive Aelynn's words."

Nautilus gripped her chin and forced her to look at him. He seemed grim and unbending, but she did not fear him. Perhaps she was growing accustomed to his touch.

"I have lost all that I thought was mine," he said in a deep growling voice that penetrated her insides with his determination. "I want sons. I have worked hard to earn a place of respect and a wife to warm my bed. My gold is worthless in this place, but I would surrender it all if you would agree to be my wife. If you cannot, then I must return to Greece and salvage what I can."

Her heart nearly failed. She had known she was not meant to be like other women, to enjoy the pleasures of the flesh, children, the love of a man. But physically knowing that she surrendered this man she desired above all others caused heart-rending anguish.

Worse, she cringed at the thought of leading the island without him. She hadn't realized how very much she depended on his experience and leadership, translating what she did not yet understand, commanding where she could not. She needed time to learn these new circumstances, and the captain would be a partner she could respect.

Hiding how she was dying inside, she bravely lifted her chin. "I dare not ask you to give up your dreams. I am not even certain that I can commit to another for the sake of the orphans. I am waiting for Aelynn to guide me."

His big hand spread across her cheek, exuding the warmth and strength she expected from him. She could almost feel his disappointment, which fed her sorrow and her pride at the same time. Not a sensible combination, she recognized. She'd been abandoned by her family when she began having visions. In her loneliness, she longed for a human touch...and to be wanted.

"We are human. You are human," he insisted. "How can Aelynn deny you the pleasures of what we are? You do realize the women who say they are committing themselves to the goddess and each other are simply finding pleasure in other women instead of men? It is only human to seek companionship, to love another more than one's self, enough to raise children and hope for a future. How can a goddess deny this comfort to her priestess?"

"Alexandra was an excellent priestess, far better than me," Tasia whispered, leaning into his hand for just this one moment of weakness. She longed to claim his reassuring support for her own, to have his hard male flesh stroking her, sharing his strength. "She did not need a man to aid her. We cannot devote our lives to two gods, and husbands demand our service."

"I won't accept that," he said angrily. "Pray to your goddess. Ask her if you cannot learn what it means to be touched and loved, as you deserve to be. To do otherwise would be a waste of all you are."

Her all too human heart yearned to believe him. As he walked away, a single tear crawled down her cheek, a tear she had not allowed since the day her parents had left her behind. It was weakness to mourn what she could not have, but it was weakness, too, to allow her heart to be torn from her chest and carried away by this mortal male.

Chapter 7

With his future at stake and with no better outlet for his physical energy, Nautilus climbed the volcanic mountain to gain a view of the vast extent of their new home. The island was worth fighting to keep, he concluded, observing the rolling expanse of lush trees and fields, hills and valleys on this side of the mountain. In time, they would need to explore the other side.

But first, he had to find a way to avoid fighting the priestess over keeping the island in a sane manner that didn't include ill-advised goddesses who would deny a beautiful woman—and himself—the opportunity for a family and happiness.

His conflict unresolved by his observations, he stomped back down, wielding his sword to cut back the jungle to create a clear path. He was a soldier, a sailor, a leader of men, not a merchant or farmer. He would have to earn his way on the sea. Still, he wanted a home of his own and a family waiting there when he returned from his journeys.

Perhaps he should look at the other maidens.

At the bottom of the mountain, as he pushed his way through banana tree fronds, he heard sobbing. He halted, and with an ear attuned to the calls of whales, located the source of the piteous cries amid a circle of flowering vines.

Pushing aside the vines, he recognized the black-haired brat who had nearly burned down the isle. The women had cut the scorched strands of the child's hair when they'd treated her. Her bowl-shaped haircut hid still healing burns.

"What are you doing away from your bed?" he asked, crouching to examine her burden.

"I got better fast," she said defensively. "Althaia did not ask me if I was well."

The child cradled a bedraggled and limp ball of feathers in her arms. He studied it with interest, and she glanced up with tearful hope. "Can you save her? I truly did not mean to kill her. I only wished to help."

That had been her excuse for setting fire to the island, too.

Frowning, Nautilus crouched down to examine the filthy creature. He had not bothered to learn the names of the sea birds that followed his ships in hopes of fish guts. He'd merely cursed their poop on his clean decks. He'd have broken the bird's neck and flung it into the sea had he stumbled upon it.

But the child's hope and tears touched his crude heart. He lifted the bird's head, received a jerk of reproof in return, and decided the creature still lived—perhaps as magically as the child. He'd never seen any person recover so quickly from burns. "She's not dead yet. Shall I carry her back to your Healer?"

The girl nodded. "She is big and weighs too much, and I think I broke her when I tried to pick her up."

The gray-white bird was indeed huge, as large as the child. Nautilus removed his chiton as he had once before for the child and formed a sling so he wouldn't maim the creature more. Tying the sling over his shoulder so the bird flapped and struggled against his back, he offered a hand to the girl. "Khaos, am I right?"

She wiped her eyes, took his hand, and nodded diffidently. "They will want you to take me away on your ship," she whispered. "I have no gift for anything except trouble. I wanted to take care of the bird all by myself so I wouldn't cause more problems."

Nautilus had to chuckle. "As far as I'm aware, all children are nothing but trouble. I once almost burned an entire ship. Sometimes, our curiosity is greater than our common sense."

She gaped at him. "Really? But Kalysta is always so good. She never gets yelled at. She studies and does as told, and Daskala loves her more than me. No one will want to adopt me."

"Did Lady Tasia tell you this?" Nautilus asked, fairly certain the priestess who had nearly died for the child would never have said such a thing.

"The priestess needs helpers, not troublemakers. That's what Daskala says," Khaos said sadly. "I am to stay on my bed and not cause any more trouble ever again."

Nautilus snorted. "We will talk to the lady about that. I can see you are not one to follow orders."

They reached the clearing where the men had erected a temporary palm-frond shelter for the women. The oven that had been built for baking bread now filled the air with delicious aromas with the grain from their supplies. Women stirred their evening meal over a fire. Children played in the sand.

And Lady Tasia was anxiously counting heads. His body responded instantly, not just to her beauty but to her concern for the littlest among them. A woman like this deserved children of her own—he desperately wanted them to be *his* children.

Her relief at seeing them approach quickly turned to sternness. She strode in their direction. Seeing the bird he carried, she rolled her eyes, and gestured for them to follow her down a separate path.

"The bird needs a Healer," Nautilus said with amusement. "And the child needs a Keeper."

For a moment, maternal concern softened the lady's expression. But the stern priestess was the one who spoke. "Althaia is this way. We will leave the bird with her. But if Khaos is well enough to wander off yet again, it's time we talk."

The girl clung more tightly to Nautilus's hand. He could no more deny her than he could give up wanting the priestess. He squeezed her small fingers. "I would like to be part of that talk, please."

Lady Tasia looked surprised but warily nodded agreement. "I don't know what knowledge you might have of children, but I suppose we should learn to work together."

They left the weakened bird with a puzzled Althaia. The priestess led them back to an opening in the hillside and gestured for them to enter.

"I've explored and found a way into this mountain with the odd walls," she explained. "I thought it might provide shelter during a rainy season. But for now, it's wonderfully peaceful."

A beam of sunlight entered from a fissure, and someone had fashioned a bench from an old tree trunk. Using a torch she'd carried from the cook fire, the priestess lit a pile of kindling, and the smoke naturally rose through an unseen opening. Nautilus admired the high ceiling and spaciousness of the chamber...and the privacy.

"Now, sit here and explain yourself, Khaos," Lady Tasia said, pointing to a low stool. "Start with why you set fire to the bluff."

"Because the ships needed a beacon," the girl said as if that were obvious. "And I'd just learned to start a fire and thought that would guide them home."

Nautilus leaned against the cave's wall and admired how the

lady gracefully adorned a crude bench as if she sat upon a throne. He bit back a laugh at the child's explanation and waited to see how the priestess would respond.

She didn't take the tack he expected.

"You knew the ships were near?"

"Yes, of course. I could hear them in my head, the sailors were so worried and tired. I thought I'd help." She sniffed and wiped a dirty cheek with the back of her hand. "I did not mean to harm you, my lady, honest. I would do anything for you. I thought you'd be happy to see the captain home."

In her *head*? The child had heard *him* in her head? Or his sailors? By Hades... Nautilus clenched his teeth and kept silent.

Lady Tasia didn't seem surprised. "Can you hear the captain now?" she asked.

Khaos shook her bobbed hair. "I can hear no one in here. It's like a magic circle. I like it. The camp is very noisy, always a loud babble, so it's hard for me to think. But the people on the ship... They were all so worried, I could sense that above all else. I couldn't hear what they said, exactly. I usually can't, so it's confusing."

The lady gently lifted the child's chin to look directly at her. "You can hear me speak now, can't you?"

The child nodded. "It's easier in here, where it's quiet."

"So the captain isn't causing any noise in your head?" The lady shot Nautilus a look that warned him not to say a word.

He was too puzzled to even think about speaking.

"Outside, the captain buzzes with too much thinking," Khaos said, eager to explain herself. "He is like a happy hive of bees, although I think he's not so happy now. I do not understand much. In here, I cannot hear him. Am I in trouble again for hurting the bird?"

"How did you hurt it?" the lady asked, wiping her thumb across a grimy cheek to remove a tear before releasing her.

"It was stealing Myra's bread, so I tried to shoo her away. But her wing was dragging and couldn't flap right. She got caught up in branches and fell, and I think I made her hurt when I tried to fix her," the girl said sadly.

The lady sighed and ran her hand through her own hair. She glanced up to Nautilus, as if he could understand more. Impatient with her strange interrogation, he removed himself from the wall and lifted the child into his arms. She was not small, but Khaos buried her face in his shoulder as if she were a toddler. He stroked her short hair.

"Am I understanding that she can hear ships from a distance but can't hear people when they are next to her?" he asked.

The lady rose and stirred the fire. "She hears *thoughts*. Can you imagine what it must be like surrounded by the cacophony of so many people thinking all day? No wonder she keeps roaming off on her own."

"That makes no sense," he argued. "One cannot hear thoughts. Perhaps she has some hearing weakness."

The lady shrugged and met his gaze without wavering. "It is possible she has some hearing impairment, too, but the one in her head is causing the most difficulty. Khaos, can you hear me speak now?"

The child on his shoulder nodded but didn't unbury her face.

"If we make a bed for you in here, would you be more comfortable?" the priestess asked.

The girl's head jerked up, and even Nautilus could read the wonder in her eyes. "You would let me stay here? With you? You will not send me away?"

"Of course I won't send you away, foolish child!" Lady Tasia came close enough to brush hair out of the girl's eyes. "You are precious to me and to Aelynn. We simply need to find a way to teach you to think before you act, and it might help if you could hear us speak."

Khaos reached for the lady, and looking uncertain, the priestess reached out to take her weight into her slender arms. The lady had to crouch down to steady her awkward burden, but she hugged Khaos's sturdy body.

Nautilus had to close his eyes against the pain of loss. Even though the lady had never known a mother, she would be a perfect one. Even if Khaos was making up her wild tale, the lady would no doubt understand why and how to correct the tale-telling. She should be rocking a babe of her own. Of *his*. How could a mere soldier persuade a goddess to give up such a treasure as her priestess?

He couldn't. He had just seen why the island inhabitants needed a priestess who understood what they were and accepted them for all their differences. He hung his head in despair. He'd only realized he had a heart after it was broken.

Chapter 8

Not entirely regretting the loss of her private hideaway but regretting the unhappiness she'd perceived in the brave captain's face, Tasia sent Khaos to gather her bedding from the camp. Perhaps the goddess consoled Tasia's loneliness by sending her a troubled child to raise.

But a child wasn't the same as having Nautilus with whom to share her concerns, Tasia realized over the next days. Newly aware of the temptation offered by his strong hand, she tried to avoid physical proximity to the captain.

Fortunately, he was busy repairing the damaged galley, so she need only avoid the harbor during the day. After a few evening meals watching him sit beside a different acolyte each night, Tasia found excuse to retreat early to her lonely cave. She should be happy that he could look to others, as she could not. Knowing he could switch so easily to another did not make her happier.

She knew he sought a wife. She had ordered the men to court her maidens. She couldn't object when he did as told. She could only suffer the pangs of the damned.

It was blunt Gaia who finally dragged Tasia from her hiding place one evening, leaving a sleeping Khaos unattended.

"I will send one of the students to watch over her," Gaia said when Tasia objected. "But you must see this, and stop it, if you can. Even Captain Nautilus seems uninterested in intervening."

"If it concerns the men, then it is not my place to interfere," Tasia argued as Gaia led her through the center of their growing village.

A student obligingly raced up the path to keep an eye on Khaos while Gaia led the way through the jungle to the bachelor's quarters.

"It is not just about them," Gaia admitted with embarrassment. "Georgós and Heron are fighting over me."

Tasia stumbled to a halt and studied her gardener's expression. She had expected the earthy Gaia to be among the first of her maidens to consider marriage, but she had thought to be consulted first. "You have given them permission to court you?"

"They did not *ask* permission," Gaia said dryly. "I have spoken with both of them over meals, that is all. Georgós is from a farming family, and he's interested in helping me grow grain and vegetables. I like him. But Heron is his senior and thinks he should have first choice, or something like that. I do not understand these male creatures."

"Nor do I, but fighting for your hand is not what I envisioned. It is your choice, not theirs." Tasia started back up the path. She could hear the shouts of encouragement now... and the clash of steel.

She would put a halt to this nonsense at once.

In the clearing where the men had formed their encampment, a fire burned. A circle of sailors surrounded the clearing. And in the center, two strong, half-naked men wielded mighty swords.

"I must admit, they are impressive animals," Gaia said with a sigh.

Bronzed skin wet with perspiration gleamed over straining muscles as the pair feinted and swung and dashed about the fire.

Perhaps she ought to be horrified that men turned against men on Aelynn's peaceful shores, but she knew these men now. No blood flowed—yet. They were disciplined soldiers. Fighting was second nature to them. And their leader would not willingly lose good men.

Did they fight themselves to weariness?

Tasia sought the captain and found him lounging in the shadows, drinking from a vessel that probably didn't contain just water. Several of the men had been experimenting with fermenting the fruits and honey they found in the interior.

"I do not have the wisdom for this," Tasia muttered, lifting her tunic from the dust and marching into the clearing. If the captain would not demand explanation, she would.

The shouts of encouragement died down as the audience grew aware of her presence. She was grateful for their respect since she had no knowledge of swordplay or how to prevent it.

It took a little longer for the heated combatants to recognize that their audience no longer cheered them on and to react to her presence. Heron took a final jab at Georgós, who swung out of danger. The would-be farmer tossed his sword into the fire, almost like a guilty child hiding evidence of mischief.

"Not a gentle maid's dream of courtship, sirs," Tasia said

sternly. Privately, she bit back her amusement at this abrupt end to the battle. She was angry at the captain for allowing the fight, but she appreciated that the men had the sense to halt when she appeared. Or perhaps it was Gaia who made them realize they were behaving badly.

The captain lazily rose from his reclining position. "We're merely establishing precedence in time-honored tradition, my lady. Have you a better suggestion?"

She heard hurt and hostility in his once respectful voice.

He was challenging *her*. He had let this fight happen so he could show she was not in charge of his men, that she could not hope to tell him or his men what to do. Horror sat like a boulder in her midsection. How did she face his challenge?

Like the combatants, the captain was half naked. His chest and arms bulged and flexed with the muscle developed over years of sailing and combat. He could easily take her if he so chose. She swallowed and could barely speak at his approach.

"Bloodshed is never the answer," she said as steadily as she could, while wishing to babble like an infant once he loomed over her. She *hated* her helplessness and that he'd take advantage of her inexperience.

She realized he not only tested her leadership—but *Aelynn's*. For Aelynn's sake, she could not let a man intimidate her with his greater size. Or let her feminine appreciation of a broad chest distract from Aelynn's purpose. The strong arms that had carried her to safety, and the brave man who had swum a sea to save her was worthy of recognition, but *he did not believe in her goddess*.

That realization hit her with the same force as the tidal wave. He could never respect her if he could not respect the goddess she represented.

In this, she did not doubt her abilities. The line had been drawn beyond which she would not go. "Weapons are unnecessary on a peaceful island," she said with the authority of her position.

"My soldiers must practice their skills if they are to defend my ships when they go trading," he countered, regarding her with the same condescending humor as she'd looked upon his men earlier.

Aelynn had made her position clear. Only believers could remain. Aelynn's position on this island was sacrosanct. This argument sailed toward a point of no return, she knew to her horror.

"Then your men must practice their skills without bloodshed," she insisted, avoiding the topic she didn't wish to broach. She glared into his eyes instead of at the vast expanse of his bare flesh. "This is Aelynn's home, and it must be a place of peace."

"We are not weaklings who cower before a woman's wishes. We are men who fight to keep what is ours." The taunt was there, in his tone. He defied Aelynn and Aelynn's priestess.

This was a moment she should have seen coming. With heavy heart, Tasia pointed to the ships in the harbor. "If you cannot recognize a greater power than your own, then you have no place among us. You may leave this isle of peace and seek a home more to your liking. Depart at dawn, and take those with you who cannot accept Aelynn's wishes."

* * *

Battening down his disbelief that the priestess would *banish* him, Nautilus grabbed her arm to drag her elsewhere for this argument.

In front of his eyes and those of his men, the priestess stiffened. Flinging off his hold, she lifted her arms, and a halo of blue light descended to envelop her, as if she'd been encompassed by a star.

His men gasped. Gaia immediately placed herself between the priestess and Nautilus, blocking him from touching the woman he wanted as his own. Nautilus clenched his fists as the fragile lady took on the aspect of icy steel.

"Only those who abide by my law shall be allowed entry to this sacred land," the priestess said in a voice not her own.

Head thrown back, arms seeking to embrace the universe, the priestess stood tall and straight inside the halo of light. Gaia dropped to her knees. So did many of his men.

Nautilus simply stared in awe at the beautiful woman who had given him reason to hope he might find a true match and a life beyond counting gold. She was far, far more than the woman he wanted for his own. *This* was the Seer the women obeyed.

The glowing figure pointed at him. "You *dare* ask for my priestess while not believing in her or me. Your arrogance and your disrespect are offensive to me and my chosen vessel. Until men recognize that the sun does not revolve around their needs, believe when you are told you have no place on this island. When you are ready to accept me, you must sacrifice as my maidens have. Cast the sword of justice into the flames and prove you are worthy of my approval. Until then, take *all* your non-believers, and depart."

The blue light vanished as if it had never been, and the priestess crumpled. Gaia stepped in to catch her, glaring at Nautilus, preventing him from coming in contact with the lady's sacred person.

Struck dumb by her words—the *sword of justice*?—Nautilus gnawed on helplessness. The lady appeared ready to collapse despite Gaia's hold, but he dared not to profane a priestess with his mortal hands after so profound a vision. His men would dismember him if the goddess did not—and they did not even grasp half of what she had said.

Battered by his desire to love and protect the woman he knew, horrified that the goddess not only existed, but did so inside this woman, Nautilus allowed the true believers to surround her. For not believing in her, he did not deserve to touch a hair of her head.

Georgós rose from his kneeling position, a look of awe upon his square face. The lowly farmer offered his arm to help the priestess, who looked too stunned and depleted to acknowledge him. Gaia nodded approval and took the lady's other arm. Between them, they led her back to the path to the village.

Nautilus swallowed his pain and nodded permission to several more of his men to accompany them. Who was he to gainsay a man's goddess?

A banished soldier, apparently. If he sailed away, how many of his men would he leave behind? They had been his family since he was a lad of twelve.

A callused, cynical man, he'd been figuratively brought to his knees by a slip of a woman—and her goddess. And oddly, he didn't wish to fight back. Some inner part of him stirred and opened to new possibilities—ones that he might not have time to explore unless he acted with swiftness and certainty. The lady had opened his heart to impossible yearning. The priestess had opened his eyes. The goddess had offered an opportunity.

He loved nothing more than exploration, except the lady.

Heron approached, a frown of puzzlement creasing his wide brow. "What does that mean, cast the sword of justice into the flames?" He glanced at the sword Georgós had tossed into the fire.

"We are all to give up our swords if we wish to stay?"

Nautilus clasped the jeweled hilt at his side, the blade that had been his constant companion as surely as the men who had raised him. He pulled the sword from his belt and showed it to his second in command. "My father gave this to me when he sent me for training. He told me I must never raise it in anger or revenge but only in defense of justice."

Heron read the characters inscribed upon it. "The Sword of Justice," he said heavily. "A real sword, not an imaginary one. Now what do we do? I have no other home but this one. I do not wish to abandon the women we have been charged to protect."

Nautilus longed to agree, but he'd been banished for his arrogance in challenging a goddess, apparently. Rightfully so. He'd thought he was challenging a mere slip of a woman. He'd been horribly, horribly wrong and deserved his punishment. Not even the lady could have known about his sword if Heron didn't.

The normally silent volcano chose that moment to shoot a shower of sparks into the midnight sky. Both men turned to observe the impressive display.

As he had the night the lady had rejected him, Nautilus suffered the ripping sensation of having his beliefs torn asunder and cast to the winds.

But a sword was stronger for having been forged of two metals. His choice was plain. He could remain unchanged, return to the man he had been and the familiar world he had known, or he could grow and learn and become stronger for his knowledge of this new place and time.

The goddess had actually offered him more hope than the priestess. She had said he could be saved, if he accepted her.

If he dared to love a priestess, he must accept that which he didn't understand—and make it work for him, as always. Staring at the sword abandoned in the dying fire, Nautilus realized that Aelynn had shown him what he must do now.

His hand curled lovingly around the sword that was all he had ever loved in this world—before Lady Tasia and her goddess had entered it.

"We start trusting in a power greater than ourselves, as the priestess commands—even if it's only the power of fellowship," Nautilus replied with new certainty. "That sounds like a solid place to start."

"The women will tell us that miracles sprout from the power of love and the goddess," Heron said gloomily.

Nautilus smiled for what felt like the first time in a long, long while. Or perhaps it only felt that way since the feeling came from deep in his heart. He'd not wanted to sacrifice what was his—until he realized that sacrifice for the greater good made everyone stronger, including himself, he hoped. He prayed the lady would approve.

"There is a difference between love and fellowship?" Nautilus asked cheerfully. "The point the lady makes is that we must think of others as well as ourselves." He shoved his sword back into its belt. "I will lead an expedition up the mountain to the fire god, if you care to join me."

* * *

After returning to her cave, Tasia sipped the strengthening drink that Althaia offered, and fell soundly asleep afterward.

In the morning, she woke to the voices of her women milling around outside her make-shift door. Khaos's bed was already empty. The welcome aroma of fresh-baked bread had apparently drawn her out.

Feeling light-headed and uncertain of exactly what had occurred the night before in the men's encampment, Tasia hurriedly dressed, wrapped her waist in her purple belt, and stepped into the sunshine.

Her maidens dropped to their knees and offered up platters of bread, fruit, and honey. Puzzled that they were not all about their tasks, Tasia gratefully accepted a bit of bread and honey and a steaming cup of herbal tea.

"I assume you have gathered here for a reason?" she asked, trying not to sound too ignorant. She was learning much of the task of leadership was knowledge and behaving as if she possessed it.

Gaia pointed at the mountain surrounded in swirls of morning mist. "The men are proving their dedication to Aelynn, as Aelynn asked."

Tasia gazed upward at the horrifying mountain and nearly choked on her tea. "They are climbing a volcano?"

"It apparently makes sense to them," Gaia replied.

Staring upward, Tasia wanted to ask if Nautilus was among the climbers, but to do so would reveal her weakness for the man she could never have, the man she had banished from her life. That much, she recalled with a pain so great it felt as if her heart had been clawed from her chest.

Through her anguish, she studied the thick green foliage. Perhaps she fooled herself, but she thought she caught a movement of white here and there, and an occasional flash of silver.

"They intend to show their dedication by falling off a cliff?" she asked skeptically, hiding her fears with pretense and by turning her face away to study the steep bare ridges above the jungle. A plume of smoke drifted lazily around the highest peak.

"By throwing their swords into the flames," Gaia explained. "The goddess told the captain he must cast his sword of justice into the fire, so they thought it would be a good thing if they all did the same."

Khaos offered a platter of neatly peeled fruit. "Georgós said you turned into a pillar of light and spoke with the voice of Aelynn. I don't want the goddess to banish the captain. He's good to me."

Tasia didn't want to banish the captain either, but she dared not question the goddess who had saved their lives and provided paradise. *A pillar of light?* She was fairly certain no former priestess had ever done anything so dramatic. No wonder the women hovered uncertainly.

"Aelynn has brought us to her home," Tasia said with a confidence she was gradually learning. "She must have done so for a reason that will be revealed with time. It seems we are closer to Her here. Have you not noticed that we are all stronger now? Let us put our strengths to following Her will and building our new home."

She glanced mountainward, still hiding her trepidation at the arduous task they'd set themselves. "And let us pray for our brave soldiers as we go about our chores."

She wanted to fall down on her knees and pray fervently until the men returned, but that would not feed the women and children left behind. Sometimes, the goddess required more practical worship.

Excitement and sheer terror built throughout the day as the men could be seen emerging from the jungle and making their way up the barren landscape near the peak. Tasia took a moment to visit the altar and pray for their safety, but what she really wanted to know was Nautilus's intentions by taking them up there.

Did Nautilus believe in her goddess now? Could he stay and learn to listen to Aelynn's laws? And if Aelynn truly accepted him and he was no longer banished—could Tasia learn to work beside him without losing sight of the goddess's desires while awash with her own?

Kneeling before the secluded altar, she studied the once-crude planks. The wood now grew lush with moss and flowers, as if an unseen hand watered and fertilized the foliage. The broad, velvety emerald planks looked more like a bed with each passing day.

She did, indeed, feel closer to the goddess in this natural bower than she had in the marble and masonry temple at home.

That evening, as the expedition neared the peak at sunset, Tasia called everyone to the altar bower so they might pray as one for the safety of the men. Surely, Aelynn would approve of the soldiers' courage, no matter how foolhardy.

Above them, the sides of the volcano glowed in a fiery red-orange that eclipsed the tropical sunset. Sirene broke into a hymn so piercing, it ought to reach the heavens, or at the very least, the mountain's peak. The murmur of prayer filled the clearing in the hush following the hymn.

Darkness descended as the men reached the furthest heights. Silhouetted against the glowing peak, Tasia saw a man stand on the brink to fling an object into the fiery depths.

The peak exploded in showers of embers that turned the night into day. The women gasped and halted their prayers to gaze in awe at the amazing show of fire. Sparks lit the heavens and molten flames seeped down the barren sides.

The men didn't flee but one-by-one, stood outlined against the flames to fling down their weapons.

Tasia wept, knowing the pride with which the men had kept their steel sharp and gleaming. Heaving the swords into the fire was akin to burning her scrolls. She didn't know if she could have done it.

The children didn't want to leave when they were chased to their beds. They stumbled down the path, glancing over their shoulders as the volcano's fiery sparks died down and the silhouettes disappeared in darkness.

There was nothing any of them could do until morning except pray that the men did not fall into the mountain's maw during the night.

Tasia stayed up well past everyone's bedtime, praying and wondering what she had done by banishing Nautilus.

Khaos fell asleep at her feet.

Chapter 9

Awed by their experience, exhausted by the day's trek down the mountainside, the soldiers collapsed in their encampment the next night. Women arrived bearing platters of food and vats of warm water for bathing—the priestess wasn't among them.

Nautilus hastily availed himself of the water and changed into a tunic not pock-marked with burnt holes from sparks. He wrapped bread and fish together and hastened down the hill.

The impossible magical metal swung weightlessly along his thigh.

He had a desperate need to talk with the lady. And to see that she was well. And... just to see her.

In the village, Gaia pointed him toward the grotto where the Healer took her patients. "Lady Tasia asked that you meet her there."

Had she been hurt and he'd not been here to help? Heart pounding in anxiety, Nautilus increased his pace through the jungle.

A single torch illuminated the grotto. In the distance, the heavenly singer's soprano reached out to the heavens. He could have sworn he'd heard her last night, when they'd been on the volcano's brink. Her voice sounded as if it came from the gods.

Now that he was on solid ground and near the sea again, he reveled in the music he'd known from birth—the blessed lap of surf and roar of waves.

No guard watched over the grotto. Frowning that the women would leave their priestess unprotected, he cautiously entered the darkness. A torch illuminated the healing pool. It took a moment for his eyes to adjust to light and shadow before he saw a woman's head bobbing above the waters, hair sleek from bathing. No Healer kneeled at the edge with her potions and herbs.

They were all alone.

Before his visit with the gods on the mountain, he would have simply strode in and presented his case like the practical, clear-eyed sailor he was. After her other-worldly speech the other night—and the results—he respected the priestess more than any king to whom he'd sworn obeisance. "May I enter?"

She glanced up, and he could swear the blue light of the goddess lingered in her eyes. She gestured for him to enter. "You have had a long journey. Join me."

He wasn't certain he heard right, so he crouched beside the pool. Holding his beloved sword across his palms, he offered the gift he'd brought down from the mountain. "Aelynn asks that I present this to you. It is no longer mine but belongs to all."

She brought up a wet hand to skim across the newly forged blade. "It is different," she said in wonder. "What happened?"

"I thought you might explain. We cast our weapons into the fire as asked. This morning, we woke to find them at our sides. But mine... This sword was changed, as the others were not. It's lighter, more flexible than anything forged by man. The hilt is now encrusted with gold and diamonds and not just the few crude gems my father could afford. But it is still inscribed by my father's words, the Sword of Justice."

She touched it reverently, then glanced to him with an expression that shook him to his very core.

"Aelynn has truly chosen you," she said in amazement. "The Chalice of Plenty is a woman's defense—the food with which to feed our children, the shelter to house our families. A Sword of Justice... this belongs to men. You will know more of its use than I."

His eyes had adjusted sufficiently to the light to see that she wore nothing. Once again, she nearly brought him to his knees. He craved so much...and not all of his desire was physical. In his lack of experience with this kind of emotion, he could not begin to separate his craving for her body from his deep need for her approval and acceptance.

But as a mere mortal man, he recognized temptation. The curves of her bare breasts floated upon the water and he was capable of understanding naught else. His body was weary but not dead.

Her words barely reached through his skull, but her tone of respect and admiration filled the emptiness that had lived inside him for too long.

Foolishly, he had once thought more respect, more gold, and a beautiful woman would provide fulfillment. This goddess floating before him had proved how very wrong he'd been about such shallow pursuits—and how much he yearned for the deeper satisfaction she could offer.

If he could only have her presence, then he'd accept whatever she offered.

Before he could ruin the moment with his crassness, he asked for his most heartfelt desire. "Like the chalice, this sword belongs to the island, as do I. I've seen your wisdom, and I'm ready to live for more than myself. May I stay?"

"You have earned the right to stay. I have asked you to join me," she reminded him. "The pool will take away your weariness. Miracles flourish all around us, and this pool is one of them. You will find it hard to sail away when the time comes."

Not certain if he was dreaming or hallucinating, fearing her last words, Nautilus hesitated. "I am still banished?"

She shook her head, and her blue gaze beckoned. "No, not at all. Aelynn has granted my wishes and given you her acceptance gift with that sword. You are not banished, but the time still comes when you must sail. Your god is the sea, and Aelynn understands that."

In his heart, Nautilus offered up gratitude to whatever power wished to accept it. "I am not certain I wish to sail away and leave you unprotected," he warned.

"We will need that which we cannot grow or make here," she reminded him. "The time will come when we must foray into the old world and exchange the gold we carried with us for items to trade and to use. We will need merchant sailors, navigators, many things. And there are those who wish to return to their families. They will not be allowed to return to the island," she said sadly.

He dipped his hand in the warm pool, longing to join her, still afraid he misunderstood her invitation. Although he began to realize why she might be making this offer—if he continued to live here, they couldn't hope to live in purity. He, at least, was only mortal, and his physical desire for her was as strong as his heart's desire. If she continued to insist on virginity, his frustration would lead to discontent.

The woman was wise beyond her years or experience.

"Our numbers will diminish once the others leave," he agreed. "But it will be easier to feed a smaller population while we build our fields."

She smiled and sank a little deeper into the water. "I have

missed our conversations. It is difficult to admit concerns to my women and still act as omniscient leader, but you always understand. I am glad Aelynn has decided to grow her worshippers from within instead of without."

She stood, rising from the waters like a sea goddess—water streaming over high breasts and erect nipples, gleaming on the nip of her waist and curve of her hip. She held out a shapely arm in a welcoming gesture. "Please, if you are still interested in me and not one of my acolytes, join me."

Her invitation could not be plainer. Hastily, Nautilus tugged at the clasp of his tunic. "I do not wish to profane you or the goddess with my humble flesh," he warned, not daring to let joy and hope take root if they were only to be trampled like tender seedlings. "If you are not saying what I hope you are, I'd rather return to my lonely bed than insult you."

"I know nothing of what is between men and women," she admitted. "I know almost nothing of men at all. But if you wish to stay, and you don't object to vows forsaking all others... I would choose you to teach me."

Astonished, Nautilus lacked the proper words to express his elation. No longer weary, his body responded as any man's would at such an invitation. But this was a virgin priestess, a woman well beyond the merchant's daughter that he had expected to take as wife. Humbled, honored, he feared her innocence would not accept his coarseness.

Standing behind a large rock, he dropped his tunic and removed his sandals. "Men are crude creatures, my lady. Look away as I climb in."

Slyly, she glanced over her shoulder just as his feet hit the water. "I have always wondered how men were different, you know. I had not realized you carried weapons between your legs."

His *weapon* extended to bursting at her admiration. Nautilus plunged into the water. He reached for her without thinking, then stopped. "Do I have permission to touch you?"

"More than permission. I have spent these nights on my knees at the altar, begging for understanding. Aelynn comes to me clearer on this magical island. I think...I believe...that we have interpreted her wishes to please ourselves in the past." She sank back to her rock again, hiding her beauty.

So as not to distract him, Nautilus thought, but he had difficulty concentrating on her words when he had permission to touch and denied himself that he might understand her change of mind and heart.

His arousal was not quenched by the warm water. In fact, the water took away his weariness and enhanced his...awareness...to an almost painful degree. He did not respond to her explanation beyond keeping his hands to himself and waiting.

"In the past," she continued hesitantly, "we have interpreted Aelynn's strictures to *be as children* to mean to be as pure as children. But here, Aelynn has it made plain to me that she wishes us to increase our numbers from within her loyal worshippers. Perhaps she has meant that we should be as children in our openness and honesty to Her. Age and cynicism blind us to those traits."

Intrigued, despite himself, Nautilus recalled Khaos and the other children diving excitedly into this new life, accepting the change without question as long as the people they knew and loved were at hand. "Perhaps She also means that we should keep our minds open? Willingly accept what the gods offer?"

She cast him a glance full of approval...and something more? Something that made his heart beat faster, like that of a child's.

"Love and trust easily," she agreed, "to be honest with each other...all those things that we discard with worldly experience. In ways, that is a far more difficult task than so basic a symbol as physical purity. Essentially, we took the easy way out by removing ourselves from the world and its temptations."

"We are still removed from the world if we stay here," he reminded her. "But it is easier to resist cynicism when we are not struggling for survival. I think I begin to understand," he said, needing time alone to ponder her theory. He could not think straight while she was naked and within arm's reach.

As if she understood, Tasia stroked his upper arm. "Now, it is up to us to show the others the path to courtship and commitment, while embracing love and trust. Are you certain this is what you want?" she asked.

"More certainly than I believe the sea rises and falls," he said fervently, finally daring to touch her chin and turn her head up to him. "Love and trust, I can offer. You have granted me all that the gods possess on Olympus. I am not certain I am worthy."

Before she could develop doubts, he bent and kissed her as gently as he knew how, hoping not to terrify her. He used only his lips to seduce her mouth, and fingers to caress her jaw, while holding back his crude body from her splendid curves.

She responded so passionately and eagerly that Nautilus couldn't resist profaning her mouth with his eager tongue, if only to lure her into repeating the gesture. She hesitated, then followed his example so thoroughly, he had to fight his baser nature to prevent treating her as if she were more experienced than she was. She was a fast student and too clever for her own good.

In her zeal, she grasped his shoulders and lifted herself closer. Being a mere male, he couldn't help wrapping his arms around her slender back and holding her in place so she could explore to her heart's content. And his. Once her kisses spun his head and her breasts pushed into his chest, he lost all ability to think clearly.

He took care not to crush her while she practiced returning his kisses. He couldn't disguise the strength of his need for her, however. She settled on his thighs and pressed his *weapon* against her belly without any apparent qualm, intent on learning the magic their mouths could create.

He'd wanted a woman of this character all his life without knowing how much until now. He'd been blind to so many things! He cupped the perfect orbs of her bottom and let the water tease around them, praying he wouldn't die of need until she was ready to take him.

"I can see that courtship requires privacy," she murmured against his mouth, while her hands explored his chest. "Khaos sleeps in my chamber with one of the students. Our people fill the shelters."

"We need a consummation temple," he laughed against her marauding kisses. "A place where we may worship with our bodies. This pool is far too rocky for what I have in mind." He brought one hand around to tease between her thighs in hopes she would understand.

She exclaimed in surprise and pleasure and eagerly rocked back and forth, demanding more. Nautilus gave her what she asked, using his fingers to soothe and excite. She responded with the need of one starved, and in his arms, she bucked and cried out with the ecstasy she'd been denied until now.

"Oh, my, I had no idea!" she gasped, collapsing in his arms and resting her head against his shoulder. "Can we do it again?" she squirmed against him, seeking more—driving him into a state of frenzy.

Desperate to have her, afraid this position would be too crude and uncomfortable for her first time, Nautilus stood, lifting her with him. She readily wrapped her long legs around his hips, and he nearly expired of need right then.

But this was a virgin lady, the goddess he worshipped, and he would learn to treat her with reverence. Well, perhaps earthy reverence.

Employing his tongue and hands to keep her willing and occupied, he carried her into the night, seeking softer grounds. He couldn't take her to his bed in the bachelor encampment, or to the blankets with the women. He should have come better prepared.

How could any man possibly prepare for bliss? Or a gift from a goddess?

Twinkling fireflies guided him down a path through the foliage. Or perhaps they were stars. He couldn't ponder miracles with soft hands running through his hair and tantalizing kisses heating his skin. She nipped his ear and tasted his jaw and returned to vanquishing his mouth with her supple tongue.

He nearly stumbled over a mossy bed in a bower enclosed by flowering vines. In relief, he offered up a prayer of gratitude and lay his...wife...upon it. This would be their marriage bed.

He climbed up to kneel over her, looking for words that would tell her how he felt, offer the pledge she required.

She ran her hands over his chest and gave him what he needed without asking. "I take thee for husband, keeper of my body and soul and father of my children, from now, until the gods decree."

Humbled by her acceptance, jubilant at the knowledge that she agreed to be the family he craved, he bent to press his brow to hers. "By Aelynn's will, I cannot take another. I take thee for keeper of my children, and as wife, keeper of my soul. I am yours to do with as you will."

Jasmine scented the air. A siren sang to the night. In the distance, the surf pounded lazily against the sand. And the volcano's fire lit the heavens. Awed by the lady's promises, Nautilus offered his thanks in kisses and caresses, teaching her the beauty and power of their bodies. With eagerness, she learned her lessons well, and returned them with the loving caresses he'd never known.

When the time came for them to join and seal their vows, Nautilus concentrated on the sound of sea and siren so he didn't rush her with his greedy demands. Instead of hesitating, she clutched his arms and raised her hips to meet him.

Tasia cried out her surprise and wonder at the pressure of fullness created by his male appendage inside her. He had grown so very large... Instinctively, she wrapped her legs around him to ease his passage, and he murmured her name in gratitude. She softened and turned liquid around him.

When he taught her how to move with the rhythm of the surf, the altar shook, and flower petals rained down upon them.

The ecstasy of release pushed her to dizzying heights, and Nautilus bellowed, shattering the night with his joy. As his seed spilled into her, a blue light bobbed before Tasia's wondering eyes. Before she could focus, the light circled and dove through her husband's loins and into her womb.

She wept with joy, and they rocked together, shuddering with the aftermath of pleasure. Tasia grasped his arms, unable to let go. When he kissed her cheeks, they were wet.

"I didn't mean to hurt you, my goddess," Nautilus murmured. "I have never experienced such...bliss and wonder... in my life. This place truly is a miracle."

She ran her hand into his hair and sighed with pleasure. "*This place* is our altar," she pointed out with a chuckle. "And I have just Seen our child planted. It will be a boy with golden hair like yours. May he be the first of many."

Nautilus bowed his head. "A family and a new world and a temple of consummation all in one night. Truly a miracle."

Tasia couldn't tell if he spoke in mirth or awe. She just knew she wasn't ready to let him go. She wriggled experimentally under him. "Surely, we must set an example for others to follow. Show me more?"

He happily obliged.

Chapter 10

Still glowing from the pleasures learned in her marriage bed, Tasia granted Gaia and Georgós courtship rights several days after she and Nautilus had shared their ceremony.

"I can give you permission to court," she warned, "but only Aelynn can bless your marriage. This is her home, and we must respect her wishes. When you are ready to take your vows, I will prepare you. The pool and the altar will be made available. After that, it's between the two of you and the goddess."

Nautilus looked up from the boards he was sawing. "I advise finding and claiming a place of your own. We may only be a small village, but privacy is hard come by."

Georgós laughed and squeezed Gaia's hand. "We have already marked a field for sowing. There is a stream that will provide water. It is lined with rocks that will build a foundation for our new home. We will need to start a list of materials to purchase when the next ship sails."

Gaia smiled shyly. "My parents were poor. I had never thought to have a husband. To have all these riches," she gestured at the lush island, "and babies, too, is well beyond anything I dared hope."

Tasia smiled in contentment as the pair wandered off. "I know this is all new and blissful, and we will have our disputes in the times ahead, but if we can just remember these moments of happiness, I think we can build a new future here."

Nautilus stood and covered her shoulders with his brawny bare arm. She didn't think she could ever get enough of his touch. She thrilled when he looked at her as he was doing now.

He kissed her forehead. "Perhaps now is the time to show you what I have found while digging our own foundation."

She glanced up at him quizzically. "Something besides dirt and rocks?"

He opened the pouch that had replaced his sword on his belt. "You may explain this in any way you wish, but I would like to think they were made for us to wear as symbols that we belong together."

He unfisted his big hand. In his palm rested two gold circlets bearing pearls.

Tasia touched them in awe. "They have a life of their own," she murmured. "How extraordinary. And beautiful." She lifted the larger band, took his left hand, and slid the ring over the finger that best fit the width. "It seems made for you."

He slid the smaller band on the same finger of her left hand. "I feel the connection between them." He bent and touched his mouth to hers. "And I want to share that connection," he murmured against her lips. "Again and again."

She wound her arms around his neck. "We have made the earth quake and the seas pound. We can do anything."

"A priestess after my own heart." He lifted her and carried her to the palm-frond tent he'd built just for them.

The cry of the seabirds and the roar of the surf joined in harmonious accompaniment with the happy cries rising from the island.

***

And so, nine months later, the first of the legendary Aelynners was born on the Mystic Isle.

Author Bio

With several million books in print and *New York Times* and *USA Today's* bestseller lists under her belt, former CPA Patricia Rice is one of romance's hottest authors. Her emotionally-charged contemporary and historical romances have won numerous awards, including the *RT Book Reviews* Reviewers Choice and Career Achievement Awards. Her books have been honored as Romance Writers of America RITA® finalists in the historical, regency and contemporary categories.

A firm believer in happily-ever-after, Patricia Rice is married to her high school sweetheart and has two children. A native of Kentucky and New York, a past resident of North Carolina and Missouri, she currently resides in Southern California, and now does accounting only for herself. She is a member of Romance Writers of America, the Authors Guild, and Novelists, Inc.

For further information, visit Patricia's network:
http://www.patriciarice.com
http://www.facebook.com/OfficialPatriciaRice
https://twitter.com/Patricia_Rice
http://patriciarice.blogspot.com/
http://www.wordwenches.com

Patricia Rice

MYSTIC GUARDIAN

A MYSTIC ISLE NOVEL

Mystic Guardian

Book View Café Edition March 11, 2014
 ISBN: 978-1-61138-359-1
Copyright © 2014 Patricia Rice
First published: New American Library July 2007
Cover illustration © Hot Damn Designs
Cover design by Kim Killion

First published by Penguin Putnam, Onyx, New York. This is a work of fiction. Any references to historical events, real people, or real locales are used fictitiously. Other names, characters, places, and incidents are the product of the author's imagination, and any resemblance to actual events or locales or persons, living or dead, is entirely coincidental.

Excerpt

More beautiful than a sun-blessed day...

As promised, the god stood on the deck of the ship, his golden hair streaming against the setting sun, the light capturing the stark angle of his bronzed cheekbones.

Awestruck, Mariel gaped and nearly stumbled to her knees at sight of Maman's promise. The filling sails accentuated the god's stance of command as the sleek ship rolled beneath his booted feet, and the sun glinted off the jeweled scabbard at his side. In billowing shirtsleeves and gold-embroidered vest, he stood head and shoulders above all the common sailors knotting lines and raising sails. The brown column of his throat emerged from the open lacing of his shirt, and Mariel thrilled at the sight. He was golden all over.

If anyone was the god her mother had predicted, that giant of a man with his air of confidence must be. Seeing him from the top of the bluff, Mariel almost wept in gratitude that once more, her mother's prophesies had come true. They were saved! Francine would eat again. The babe would be born healthy. All would be well...

And then—as she waved a greeting and raced for the path leading down to the beach—he turned away to watch the ship's sails unfurl to catch the wind and outgoing tide.

Waves of despair and fury washed over her. *He couldn't leave! The golden god was supposed to save Francine.*

Standing on the bluffs above the harbor, Mariel choked on a half sob as the wind licked at the canvas. Hunger brought her emotions too close to the surface these days, and she wrestled with her failure now.

The cries of the gulls wailed her dismay.

Maman's predictions were *never* wrong. She had promised a golden god would save the village from straits most dire. Not a single person in the village would survive if their situation became any more desperate.

She was the only one who could act on Maman's predictions. It was her task to do so—but she'd arrived too late to prevent the ship from sailing.

No, she hadn't. She'd been here on time. The wretched man simply refused to wait! More must be required of her.

With the force of terror driving her, she scrambled over the rocks.

***

On this, his last journey into the world outside his own, Trystan l'Enforcer admired the cliffs of Brittany without a trace of regret. He was looking forward to the responsibility awaiting him, the one for which he'd prepared all of his life.

Behind him, the sails of his pride and joy, the *Sword of Destiny,* unfurled in preparation for catching the tide that would, for once and all, carry him home. No more wandering the sea.

Oddly, at this moment of rejoicing, a poignant cry of defeat carried over the wail of the wind, a cry that reached deep down inside as if to draw him back to the shore. With the wind whipping his hair, he scanned the scene for the source of the sound, and was arrested by the sight of a Breton maiden atop the bluff, waving her farewells. Her cap a lacy crown against her ebony hair, she wore long black skirts and a pristine white apron, identifying her as a simple villager, unlike the richly dressed merchants with whom he often dealt. He had learned many things about modes of dress in countries other than his own, things he must pass on to his nephew, who would sail the *Destiny* once Trystan married and took his place on the Council.

"Now there's a lass someone has made happy." Nevan l'Nauta, his navigator and closest friend, watched the willowy girl shout and wave from the path. "Can you read lips in that language? What does she say?"

"She tells us to wait," Trystan replied, his gaze not wavering from the comely wench. "She needs to speak with us." He stood at the rail, boots spaced widely, adjusting to the swell and fall of the sea as the wind tugged his shirtsleeves and blew the maid's words away.

The tide was on the way out. This was the moment he reveled in—when ship, man, and sea became one, and home became more tangible than a thought.

There was no chance of waiting, even for this comely miss.

But for some inexplicable reason, he could scarcely tear his gaze from the words tumbling from her mouth, as if an invisible tether had bound his eyes to her lips. And to her nimble figure as she frantically scrambled down the rocks, calling...

Abruptly, the wind stilled, abandoning the sails with a single loud slap of the canvas, as if it, too, felt the tension of her call and dared not interfere.

"What is happening?" cried a crewman from the rigging, puzzled by the sudden calm.

With trepidation, Trystan wrenched his gaze from the vision on the cliff to search the sagging canvas and the clouds above. Nothing marred the perfection of blue sky and wave. What sorcery was this?

The cries from shore merged with that of the gulls above and the sea creatures below, calling him to turn back...

Nonsense, Trystan snarled in denial, setting his shoulders, resisting the call. His future lay ahead, on the beautiful isle he called his home. The wind did not stop and the gulls did not cry for him, but for a caprice of nature. The woman was a mere distraction.

Without warning, the canvas again filled with a stiff breeze, seeming as eager as he to be off. Or more like, her captain, Waylan Tempestium, had stirred the winds. Dismissing the maiden's futile cries, Trystan crossed his arms, leaned his hip against the rail, and forced his thoughts back to the future. "Despite the charm of Brittany's maidens, I'm eager to return to the black sand of Aelynn," he said with firm assurance.

"Are you missing the sand, or Lissandra?" Nevan responded with a laugh. "If absence makes the heart grow fonder, she should be on the beach, waving you home."

Trystan tried to picture cool, enigmatic Lissandra waving joyfully—or even furiously—like the maid on the bluff, and could not. "If she makes room for me at the dinner table, I will be grateful. We are of like mind."

"You both love our island home and wish to guide its future," Nevan agreed.

Trystan caught another glimpse of the woman on shore. She had lifted her skirts to scramble down the path, revealing fine ankles. He wished he had been the lucky man who'd wooed her in their brief hours in this coastal village.

He shook his head sharply to dislodge his whimsy. As a man driven by his sense of duty, he'd resisted the ladies on this short journey. Given her gift as a Seer, Lissandra was bound to know if another woman held his thoughts, and her stubborn nature would require that he pay—with great pain, no doubt. He grinned, imagining the path of his intended's revenge, even as he continued to watch the lass clamber expertly down the rocky path, shouting and gesturing.

The increasing wind blew the flaps of his vest, tugging his hair loose from its binding, and he swayed with the roll of the rising waves. "Maybe some other time, fair one," he shouted, although he knew she could not hear over the roar of the breakers.

"You don't think one of our men has made her promises?" Nevan asked with interest as the lithe dynamo grabbed boulders and slid on wooden sabots to the sandy shore, as if she would dive in after them.

Did he mistake, or had she just called him a rude name? Judging by the way she shook her fist, he assumed those weren't pleasantries she was hurling.

"It wouldn't be the first time, nor the last." Trystan sighed his regret as the beautiful creature ran down the beach through the foam, her skirts up to her knees, exposing shapely calves. "We all know we must choose carefully, but she seems hale and hearty enough, if a bit thin. Ask around, see if her suitor left sufficient coin to last her until next time. From all reports, they've had drought this past year, and the harsh winter has driven the fish away."

He watched as the lass caught the cap falling from her loosened hair and flung it down, stomping it into the wet sand.

"Her hair is the black of Aelynn's sands." Trystan nodded at the furious female. Then fighting this odd longing for that which he could not have, he deliberately turned and walked away. He was going home. For him, that was freedom—freedom to finally begin his future as he would have it.

He had been groomed since birth for the privilege and power of a princedom that did not exist to the Outside World. For the good of all, it must remain that way. His home wasn't called Aelynn, the Mystic Isle, for naught.

***

Mariel's heart sank in despair as the ship joined the tide despite her hasty scramble and cries for a halt.

She refused to accept another day of watching the village die. Her mother's prophesy had to be true. If still more were required of her, then more she would do. She had never attempted such an impossible goal as the one before her, but if this was the last thing she ever did, she could not let the ship escape without her.

She seldom dared indulge her gift in daylight, but she would risk all for this.

Made in United States
Cleveland, OH
09 July 2025

18384748R00056